TOMBS
OF BLUE ICE

TOMBS
OF BLUE ICE

by RON FAUST

A BLACK BAT MYSTERY

THE BOBBS-MERRILL COMPANY, INC.
Indianapolis / New York

M ✓

ISBN 0-672-52011-7
Library of Congress catalog card number 74-6523
Designed by A. Christopher Simon
Manufactured in the United States of America

First printing

TOMBS
OF BLUE ICE

1

We were only three hundred feet below the summit when the storm finally broke. It was two o'clock on Saturday afternoon. The air had a chemical odor. There was a humming of static electricity, and St. Elmo's fire flickered bluishly around our metal equipment.

We had noticed the storm building through the morning hours and at eleven o'clock had paused for a consultation. I wanted to continue. Cottier was in favor of a retreat. Streicher, the youngest and least experienced, said he would abide by any decision that Cottier and I reached.

I argued that the storm was still a few hours away and that we could certainly reach a point near the summit before it broke. Most of the difficult climbing would be below us then. This was probably only a brief afternoon storm. It might snow for a couple of hours and then clear by evening. Even if it did not clear we could bivouac tonight and next morning push on to the summit, through bad weather if necessary. Actually, I said, if we moved fast we could probably make the summit before the storm hit us.

"I don't know," Cottier said.

From the summit it was a relatively easy descent to the refuge on the northwest ridge.

"Look at that sky," Cottier said. "I don't know."

Today was the first of September. The season was almost over; we might not be able to do any more climbing this year.

"Well," he said, "if we go all out. . . ."

"You decide, Etienne. We can start rappelling down to the glacier now or we can blitz the summit."

"All right," he said. "Let's go on."

"Dieter?"

"Let's get moving, then," Streicher said.

We climbed swiftly, using a minimum of pitons and belays, but we lost an hour through poor route-finding and clumsy rope-management. If not for that lost hour we might have been on our way down the ridge when the storm hit.

During the last few pitches we could hear thunder and see lightning stab through the dark clouds. We kept climbing, and then we were in it.

We had just enough time before the storm struck full force to prepare our bivouac site: a few pitons to which we tied ourselves and our rucksacks; a moment to put on our down jackets and waterproof ponchos, just enough time to arrange ourselves in moderate comfort on the nine-foot-long, three-foot-wide ledge. That ledge was a

RON FAUST

beautifully horizontal piece of terrain compared to the
rest of the vertical rock wall. Cottier and I sat on the ends;
Streicher was between us.

"The air stinks," Cottier said. "We're going to get some
lightning."

"Do you want to put all the metal stuff in a rucksack
and lower it over the side?" I asked. But there was no
more time.

The mists swarmed around us and small hailstones
began to rattle off the rock. There were flashes of lightning
which expanded into huge spheres that illuminated the
mist like sun shining behind a cloud, and these were followed by the peals of thunder. One detonation lasted for
more than ten seconds. It went off like a munitions factory
or oil refinery blowing up and then continued to rumble
and crackle and reexplode until all three of us were
shouting with fear.

The expanding balls of light were all around us in the
mist, some far out, just small brightly glowing spheres,
and some closer, and these illuminated everything with
a pale shuddering glow. Bright tentacles snaked through
the smoky atmosphere. When the thunder was close I
could feel the concussion in my abdomen. My mouth was
dry and tasted bitter.

We were in the worst of it now. There was a crackling
and buzzing in the air, a throbbing hum of static electricity.
The pitons and ice axe heads sputtered with bluish green
light. Our woolen hats discharged sparks, and beneath
the hats our hair bristled. A tiny blue flame danced around
the metal rims of Streicher's sunglasses. We all shouted.
It came then, a blinding flash of light, close above us, a
brilliant quivering glare, and then the resonant explosion.

3

I was knocked unconscious. I awoke dangling from my piton cord. My head felt as though it were filled with carbonated water. I pulled myself back onto the ledge.

Silence now, although the mist still vibrated with the glowing and shrinking spheres and the jagged stabs of lightning. Mist billowed around us and condensed on the black rock. There was a coppery taste in my mouth. The air stank of ozone. Gradually my hearing returned. I could hear thunder, muted still, and a faint droning noise —my own voice. I was talking aloud. But my ears felt stuffed with putty; I could not understand the words and my mind refused to reveal their meaning to me. And so I talked without ever knowing what I said.

Streicher and Cottier had been knocked off the ledge too. They hung limply at the ends of their safety cords. Both seemed to be unconscious but Streicher was groaning softly. I lengthened my own safety cord and slid down the ledge until I was just above Cottier. His head was level with the rim of the ledge. He faced down toward the glacier with his head lowered in an attitude of penitence. His eyes were open. I reached down and pressed my index finger against his eyeball. There was no reflexive response.

Cottier's hat was gone and his fair hair was blackened and smoking. The lightning had entered at the base of his head and exited through his right knee. The wool knickers were blackened and smoking, too. I could smell burned fabric and burned hair and I could still smell the bitter chemical odors of the storm.

Lightning flashed through the blowing mist. Thunder shook the mountain. My hearing had not completely re-

4

turned and the thunder sounded dull and remote, like the artillery of armies fighting somewhere over the horizon.

Streicher was gradually regaining consciousness. His eyelids fluttered and he spoke softly in German. His voice had a querulous tone, like the voice of an old man who was resigned to everything but still complained out of habit. I lay flat on the ledge and looked at him. There were burns on his face, and his hair had been singed down to the scalp on one side. An area of his nylon poncho had been melted.

"Dieter?" I called.

His eyelids fluttered.

"Dieter!"

His eyes opened. The pupils were tiny black dots. I watched the dots and when they had dilated I asked, "Are you badly hurt?"

"My leg," he said. "Oh, Christ."

"We've got to get you back up on the ledge."

"Jesus," he said. "Be careful of my leg, Holmes." Streicher usually spoke English beautifully but now there was a thick accent.

"Help me, Dieter," I said. "I don't know if I can get you up here by myself."

He helped me as much as he could and did not faint until his torso was resting on the ledge. His fainting then made the rest easier for both of us, since there was no way I could get his lower body up onto the ledge without abusing his bad leg. I handled him as if he were a sack of potatoes or a store mannequin. I got him onto the ledge and turned him over on his back. His right leg was broken midway between knee and groin. I could hear

5

the bone ends grind together when I straightened the leg. Those ends had undoubtedly torn through a lot of muscle and tissue, but at least the fracture remained simple; bone had not penetrated skin.

I could not understand how his leg had been broken. The femur is a very strong bone, and he had not fallen more than a couple of feet before the safety cord had stopped him. There should not have been any great strain or blow on his leg. The concussion of the lightning had been tremendous, but I could not see how it would break that one bone. There was no figuring it. It was just one of those freak accidents.

I had to splint the leg before Streicher became conscious again. He was lying supine on the ledge and I did not have much room to work in. I could not have set the leg properly even if I had been competent to do so; but I could splint it and that way protect it from further damage, and maybe prevent an involuntary muscle contraction from driving a sharp bone end through the skin. I used two ice axes for the splint and wrapped them tightly with tubular nylon cord.

The storm was receding toward the south now. The lightning appeared dimmer; the thunder no longer vibrated inside me. The clouds remained and snow ticked softly against the rock. There did not seem to be any more danger from lightning. Lightning can strike twice in the same place. It very often will. Once, twice, again and again. But not today.

The lightning that had killed Cottier had discharged above us, and either the main or a subsidiary bolt had traced a path of least resistance down the rock. It was Etienne's misfortune that he happened to be occupying

6

that path. He was dead and Streicher was injured and I had received a terrific jolt.

Streicher groaned. His hands clenched and unclenched convulsively. After a minute his eyes opened.

"How are you?" I asked when his eyes had cleared.

"I've felt better."

"A lot of pain?"

"It's pretty bad. How is Etienne?"

"Dead."

"It's snowing," he said.

"The summit isn't far. I'll climb out of here tomorrow morning and get a rescue party together. We'll have you down in the valley by tomorrow night, or Monday noon at the latest."

"Holmes, have you got any morphine?"

"No, but maybe there's some in Cottier's rucksack." There was. I found a hypodermic syringe and three morphine ampoules in his first aid kit. Etienne had always been a well-prepared climber; it was just that there was not much you could do to prepare for electrocution.

I gave Streicher an injection of morphine, and after a time his voice became drowsy and almost contented. We talked and then he fell asleep.

I went through Cottier's rucksack and removed a wedge of cheese, a few rounds of sausage and a half bottle of red wine. We had intended to drink the wine at midday but then had omitted lunch in our race against the storm. I drew the cork and drank directly from the bottle. It was bad wine demanding sanctuary behind a good label. I drank the wine and ate the cheese and sausage and then drank some water.

It was snowing heavily now, big wet disks that fluttered

endlessly downward. Because of the falling snow and the cloud, I could see no more than forty or fifty feet in any direction.

My watch had stopped at exactly 2:33. The watch operated on an electric cell, and apparently the lightning had blown it out. I guessed that the time was about 3:30. I lit a cigarette and sat back to wait out the storm.

The avalanches started at around 6:30. The rock wall above us was so steep that the avalanches were triggered before a dangerous amount of snow could accumulate. They came hissing down the face, powdery curtains of snow that poured past the ledge on down toward the glacier below. Snow piled up on the ledge and filtered through my clothing. Every now and then I brushed the snow off the sleeping Streicher. The force of the snow-falls moved Cottier's dangling body. His hair and shoulders were powdered white. These avalanches were no problem, but I could hear the dull thud and river-rapids roar of the big ones sweeping down a nearby couloir.

It stopped snowing at about ten o'clock that night. The avalanches continued for a while, and then it was quiet. The cold would come now. I removed my down jacket and covered Streicher with it. That left me with a heavy wool shirt, a sweater and the light nylon poncho. I emptied a rucksack and drew it up over my feet and lower legs. I drew on my mittens. I pulled my woolen stocking hat down over my ears and forehead. The mists thinned, vanished. A few holes appeared in the clouds above and I could see stars shining coldly against the blue black of the sky. Gradually the whole sky cleared. The Milky Way shone like dense and luminous powder.

I slept for a time, and then the cold awakened me. It

was a fierce, penetrating, steel-hard cold. The moisture in my nostrils froze. My lungs burned. The cold went through me like a continuous electrical current.

Dieter woke and asked me for another injection of morphine.

"Maybe you should eat something," I said.

"I can't eat."

"Dieter, we've only got two ampoules left."

"Give me one. Please, Holmes."

I gave him another injection.

The mountain softly creaked and groaned in the silence. Other mountains were darkly silhouetted against the star-sprayed sky. Far below me I could see the phosphorescent shine of the glacier. The night had a cold, hard mathematical beauty.

2

Finally the sky paled: a dirty gray light that slowly changed to a glossy pearl shade. The sky turned blue, and long indigo shadows reached across the glacier. The surrounding mountains were clean and white with new snow against the dark blue of the sky. Streicher was still sleeping. His face was pale and there were dark crescents beneath his eyes.

I drank a little water and then rose stiffly to my feet. The climbing would not be easy. The rock wall was patched with brittle black ice. Snow had collected on every wrinkle and filled every crack. It would be difficult to do free-climbing, but I had slings and sufficient pitons, and so I could climb it artificially if necessary. And if I could not safely ascend I would rappel back down to the glacier.

I collected all the food and water from our rucksacks and placed it near Streicher. I left a little Primus stove too, in case he wanted to boil water for tea. Then I made certain that he was secure on the ledge: there was not too much slack in his safety cord; the piton was solidly placed; the knots were tight. Everything would be fine until the rescue party arrived.

I looted the rucksacks of spare pitons and karabiners and then stood quietly waiting. It seemed to me that something vital had been forgotten. I went through a mental check list: pitons, karabiners, crampons, slings, a one-hundred-and-twenty-foot coil of eleven-millimeter rope, piton hammer, ice axe. Something was missing. I scooped a double handful of snow from the ledge, packed it into a snowball and began sucking on it. What had I forgotten? Then it occurred to me that what I had forgotten was Cottier. My unconscious had been waiting for him. But of course he was dead, and the cold and rigor mortis had turned him into something that resembled a piece of marble statuary.

"Dieter," I said. "Dieter."

He opened his eyes and looked up at me. "Going now?"

"Yes."

"Good luck, Holmes."

"Thanks. How do you feel?"

"Like I've been hit by lightning and have a broken leg."

"I've left you plenty of food and water."

"I'll be all right."

"Sure."

"You'd better take your down jacket," he said.

"You keep it."

"No, the sun will get around to this side of the mountain pretty soon. It will warm up. You take it."

I lifted the down jacket off his chest and put it on.

"How long do you think it will take?" he asked.

"It's about six now. With any luck I should reach the refuge in five or six hours. If there are any climbers there, we'll come right back up and get you. Otherwise, I'll go straight down to the valley and organize a group. We should be able to get one of the French Army helicopters. Either way, we'll have you out of here by tonight, or tomorrow morning at the latest."

"That's good."

"And listen—if something should happen to me, don't worry. Martigny knows what climb we were doing, and if we don't show up he'll get a rescue party together. It may take a little longer that way, but they'll get you out of here."

"You'll make it all right," he said. "Listen, Holmes. Give me the last of the morphine."

"Do you need it now?"

"No, but I will in a couple of hours. Anyway, I don't know how to give an injection. Give it to me now and when that wears off I'll get by."

I gave him the morphine injection, then stood up again and shouldered my rucksack.

"I could get to like that stuff," he said.

There was a smooth bulge of rock above the ledge. It could have been negotiated free-climbing under ordinary conditions, but the ice and snow doubled every difficulty. I searched the rock for a crack, found one, reached up with my piton hammer and chipped away the ice until the crack was clear. I drove in a long angle piton. The shock traveled up my wrist and forearm. The clear metal-to-metal ringing changed pitch with each blow. It rose higher and higher until it began to approach the limits of human hearing. I buried the piton to the eye and clipped on a karabiner and sling. The sling was made out of nylon webbing and had three footloops. I stepped into the bottom loop. Two more steps and I had gained about four feet of height. I cleared away more of the brittle ice and drove another piton into the same crack. Attached another karabiner and sling. Stepped into that sling and awkwardly leaned down and removed the first set. I proceeded this way, building a stairway of short ladders up the overhang. It was the graceless, drudging bastard-child method of conventional mountaineering.

"Luck, Holmes," Streicher said.

The morphine was working now and his voice was slurred; the German accent had returned.

There were some steep granite slabs above the over-hang. If the rock had been dry I would have free-climbed upward, using the delicate friction holds. I might even have tried it now in crampons if I had not been alone. With a couple of safety pitons and a good belay from below it would have been reasonably safe. But I was alone and so I continued climbing by artificial methods, hammering in one peg after another and moving up the slings.

The slabs went on for about thirty meters, and then the rock was shattered into huge blocks. The holds were larger and more numerous now. I strapped on my twelve-point crampons and easily traversed leftward some fifty meters to the base of a vertical chimney. The chimney looked fairly simple. It was choked with ice and snow, but the rock was well broken and there were small ledges and spurs of rock that would serve for hand and footholds.

The chimney was about twenty meters high and funneled open onto a chaotic tumble of loose granite blocks. The angle decreased to about sixty degrees. The shattered blocks led to an ice slope, and I cramponed directly up to the summit.

It was a surprise, as always, to leave the physical world behind and stand free in the sky. There was a feeling of liberation, of transcendence, but the emotion was tinged with a vague sense of annihilation, too. It is when you are most alive that you become most aware of death.

The sky was a dark, luminous blue. Mountains thrust their jagged white noses into the blueness in a 360-degree arc. I picked out the Matterhorn and Monte Rosa, the Bernese Oberland group, the Mönch, the Eiger and the Jungfrau, and I could see most of the great peaks and spires here in the Mont Blanc massif. The Aiguille Verte, the Dent du Géant, Mont Blanc itself, all seemed to be within spitting distance in the clear mountain air. Every major peak was shining in the sunlight, but the valleys were still obscured with lavender mist and shadow.

I wanted to get off the mountain while it was still cold. Avalanches would begin again when the sun warmed the snow.

The ridge was steep and corniced for about a thousand vertical feet and then it broadened and the angle decreased. I continued down through the knee-deep powder snow. Far below I could see the mass of enormous boulders which protected the refuge from avalanches.

There was a man sitting on a rock in the sun. He was smoking a pipe and looking up toward me. When I was lower I could see that it was Jules Martigny, the retired guide who was the hut guardian and the man who owned the pension in the valley where Cottier, Streicher and I stayed. In fact, it was Martigny who had recommended yesterday's climb to the three of us. I descended to the small plateau and removed my rucksack.

Martigny chewed on the stem of his pipe and looked at me for what seemed a long time. "The others?" he asked finally. "Cottier?"

"Dead. He was struck by lightning yesterday afternoon."

He nodded slowly. "And the German?"

"He has a broken leg. He's on the ledge one hundred meters below the summit."

"So," Martigny said. He got up from the rock and brushed the snow off his trousers. "I have soup and wine, if you don't mind that for breakfast."

"Jules," I said, "Streicher has to be taken off that ledge and down to a hospital."

"Of course."

"Are there any climbers here?"

"None."

"Then perhaps you and I—"

"What? Just the two of us? One man to descend on ropes with the stretcher and the other to haul him and the German up to the snow field beneath the summit?"

"I could go down and strap Streicher into the stretcher, climb up to you and together we could pull him up."

"And leave an injured man helpless and unattended on a stretcher? To swing this way and that like a clock pendulum, to twist in the air, to get jammed beneath an

16

overhang? You are agitated and not thinking clearly, my friend. You know better. It will be necessary to have at least five or six good men, and maybe a spool of cable and a winch."

I thought about it for a moment and saw that he was right. I nodded. "Okay. I'll go down to the valley and organize a rescue party."

"Certainly you will. But first you'll eat a little hot food. You've had a bad night. Ten or fifteen minutes' delay won't matter. The rescue party will probably obtain use of an army helicopter. The helicopter can land right over there, you see? They've done it before. The German will be safe in a hospital bed sometime tonight."

"I don't know," I said.

"Do as I say. I know a little more about these things than you." He turned and started through the snow toward the refuge.

I followed him into the refuge, a long stone building with a sun deck and a steep shake roof. I left my ice axe and rucksack in the foyer rack and went inside. There were twenty bunks in two tiers around the room, and a small kitchen space.

I sat down at the table and watched Martigny as he moved about, preparing the food.

He used his hands well considering how badly they'd been mutilated. Some years ago, while he was involved in a rescue attempt on the Col de la Brevna, Martigny's hands and feet had been severely frostbitten. Dry gangrene had set in, and after a series of amputations all he had left were knobby, rounded stubs for fingers. Both thumbs were intact, but all the fingers had been amputated at either the first or second joint, and now his hands looked more

17

like thick, horny talons than anything human. He'd lost all of his toes, too, and so he wore boots that were shaped like small boxes. I'd heard that he was still a fair climber, but of course he could no longer earn his living as a guide.

If I were making movies, Martigny would be the man I'd typecast to play an old outdoorsman. He was short, but very broad and powerful, like a bear. His hair and eyebrows were pure white and contrasted sharply with the tobacco-brown coloring of his face, which was lined and pocked, scoured by wind and sun and cold. His skin had actually been tanned into leather while he still lived.

Now he carried two big steaming bowls of soup to the table and then made another trip for a block of Gruyère cheese, salt, pepper, butter, a loaf of brown-crusted bread and a bottle of red wine. He sat down across from me, muttered grace in French, then took his knife and shaved thin flakes of cheese into his soup. The cheese formed a bubbly, viscid layer which he then sprinkled with salt and pepper. He cut off a slab of bread, spread it thickly with butter, dipped it into his soup and began eating. After a moment he looked up at me. "Do my peasant table habits disgust you?"

"No," I said.

"Aren't you hungry, then?"

"No. I thought I was, but I'm not."

"Eat a little," he said. "See if your appetite doesn't return."

I took two spoonfuls of the soup and a bite of bread and then I was ravenous. We ate everything and drank all the wine.

Afterward Martigny cleared the table and returned with the climbing log. He opened it to a blank page and

18

set the book and a ball-point pen in front of me. Then
he got out his pipe, stuffed it with tobacco, lit it and
sat quietly smoking. When the pipe was empty he tapped
out the ashes and scraped the bowl with a penknife.

"Don't you want to make an entry in the log?" he asked.

I picked up the pen, wrote the date and then: "Etienne
Cottier was killed yesterday at 2:33 P.M. by lightning
while climbing the North Face. *Dum vivimus, vivamus.*"

The old man took the book, turned it around and read
my entry. "What does that mean? *Dum vivimus, vivamus?*
Something about life?"

"While we live, let us live."

Martigny drew a large cross on the page so no one else
could make an entry there. "The mountains can be cruel,"
he said. "I sometimes wonder why we fool with them."

"Because living in the anthill is crueler."

"Go directly to the police," he said. "Report the accident. They will notify the people at the guide head-
quarters."

"All right," I said.

"Do you know the way down? Follow the ridge to a
very big talus slope. It may be snow-covered now, but I
don't think there will be any danger of avalanches, not
for another two or three hours. At the base of the talus
there is a huge rock, bigger than my chalet. You'll pick
up the trail there."

I thanked him, paid for my breakfast and went outside.

3

The forest was greenly cool and smelled of pine resin and decaying wood. Trees near timberline were powdered with snow but there was no snow lower down. The woods were on a steep mountain and the path zigzagged down in long traverses. I descended another thousand feet and then the woods opened out into some rolling meadows. It had rained here yesterday and the grass was still wet and had a lacquered gloss in the sun. Drops of water became tiny prisms and flashed amber and violet and crimson. Bright alpine flowers were scattered like coins over the meadow. Beyond a low hill I could hear the gentle chiming of a cowbell.

I walked down a series of meadows to the valley and a town. There was a crosshatch of narrow streets with shops and cafés and small hotels and a grim stone church. The church bells clanged as I walked past. Tourists wan-

21

dered up and down the streets, and one of them took a photograph of me. I kept walking. This was one of a number of small tourist and farming communities scattered throughout the miles-long Arve River valley. The largest town, Chamonix, was located about midway between the passes at the east and west ends of the valley. Mountains rose steeply to the north and south.

The Préfecture and the office of the Company of Guides were in Chamonix. I did not want to wait for the electric train that serviced the valley and so I walked through town, crossed a bridge over the river and stood on the side of the main road. This was the last big tourist weekend until ski season and there was considerable traffic. After I spent a few minutes thumbing, a pickup truck carrying three people stopped for me. There wasn't room in the cab and so I jumped over the tailgate and sat on a bale of hay in the back.

I smoked a cigarette and watched the country unravel. The road paralleled the river for a while, and then it crossed over to enter Les Chosalets. I got a glimpse of the Argentière glacier through a narrow gap in the mountains. We passed through Le Grassonet and then Les Tines and then a little later we curved into Les Praz. We crossed the river again. Around Les Praz I could see a part of the great Mer de Glace glacier. It was steep and broken, mostly a dirty gray in color, although here and there I saw flashes of sea-green and cobalt-blue.

We ran alongside the north bank of the river into Chamonix. The truck stopped for a light near the center of town. I thanked the driver, picked up my rucksack and jumped out.

Chamonix was scattered on both sides of the Arve. It

was a fair-sized town built in a variety of architectural styles—Tudor, baroque, Gothic, cuckoo clock, international Hilton, rustic. . . . The streets were crowded with tourists and climbers.

I went directly to the Préfecture. Inside, a policeman, sitting behind a huge larchwood desk, looked up as I entered the room. A girl was typing at a smaller desk in the corner and a half dozen people sat on benches against the east wall.

"I want to report a climbing accident," I said to the policeman.

"If you will sit down over there," he said.

"One of the men is injured, but alive."

The policeman stared at me for a moment, nodded, got to his feet and led me down a narrow hallway. He knocked on the door, paused, knocked again, and then, without waiting for a response, pushed it open. He beckoned me into the room and closed the door behind me.

A tall, beefy man stood up from his desk. "Do you speak German?" he asked me in that language.

"No."

"English, then?"

"Yes, but I also know French."

"That's all right, we will speak English. I am Captain Guillot."

"Robert Holmes." We shook hands.

"Sit down, please. I will be only a moment."

I sat in a chair opposite his desk. It was the standard police station: drab, functional, impersonal. They are basically the same throughout the world; this one could just as easily have been located in Chicago or Istanbul or Madrid. It had the obligatory scarred desk, the green metal filing cabinets, the hard chairs, a calendar, a telephone, an electric floor fan, and a big cylindrical waste basket.

"Now," Captain Guillot said, looking up from his papers. We politely studied each other. He was big for a Frenchman, big for any nationality, about six foot four and two hundred and forty pounds. He had very pale blue eyes and mismatched lips. His upper lip was thin and finely curved, like a girl's; his lower lip was thick and red and pendulous. I wondered if somewhere there might be a girl with a beautiful lower lip and a heavy blood-gorged upper one. His eyebrows had a satanic slant. The eyebrows and mouth made him appear to be constantly, silently laughing at you.

"There's been an accident in the mountains," I said. "One man is dead and the other is injured."

"Did you just come down from the mountains?"

"Yes."

"Would you like a drink, then?"

"Yes, please."

He went to the metal filing cabinet, pulled open a drawer and withdrew a decanter and two cordial glasses. He poured both glasses to the brim and passed one of them over the desk. It was very good plum brandy. I lit a cigarette.

The Captain sat down at his desk. He tugged at his thick lower lip with a thumb and forefinger for a moment and then he looked at me. "One dead, one injured. I assume they both are still in the mountains."

"Yes."

"We will have to get them down from there, won't we?" He picked up the telephone and in French told whoever answered to arrange to have one of the guides come immediately to his office. He replaced the receiver. "Now," he said. He searched through his drawers, found a sheet of paper and inserted it into an ancient typewriter. "Your name in full."

"Robert William Holmes."

The typewriter clattered. "You are an American, Mr. Holmes?"

"Yes."

"Your occupation?"

"None at the present."

"How do you live?"

"Frugally."

"What do you do when you work?"

"Whatever is available. A little carpentry, bartending, some free-lance journalism occasionally. In the winter I teach skiing."

"You're a mountain bum, then. Excuse the expression."

"I suppose you could say that."

"One of those happy vagrants. Well, all right. How old are you, Mr. Holmes?"

"Thirty-five."

"Your address?"

"I'm staying now at the Martigny pension."

"You must be comparatively solvent now. Most of our mountain bums—excuse the expression—live the summer in tents. What is your permanent address?"

"I have none at the moment."

"How long have you resided in France, Mr. Holmes?"

"Six years."

"Where is your passport?"

"At the pension."

He attacked his typewriter with two fingers. He typed

rapidly and for some time, stopped, made an erasure and typed over it.

"What was the nature of the accident?" Captain Guillot asked.

"Lightning. Etienne Cottier was killed. A man named Dieter Streicher has a broken leg. I don't know how it happened."

"Streicher," he mused. "Streicher. . . . I suppose there are many Streichers in Germany and Austria."

"I don't know."

He attacked the typewriter with a kind of melancholy rage. "What time did the accident occur?"

"At about 2:30 yesterday afternoon."

"Where exactly?"

I told him.

He typed for a moment more and then leaned back in his swivel chair. "This has been a very bad weekend. There were a great many climbers in the mountains when this storm developed. Some climbers are stuck on high rock walls, unable to ascend or descend. They must be rescued. There have been lives lost in avalanches, icefalls, rockfalls . . . and simple falls. And lightning. Tomorrow we will hear about more deaths. From exhaustion, exposure, avalanches, icefalls, rockfalls, crevassefalls, and simple falls. Right now there are dozens of people who are in trouble in our mountains. Everyone is trying to help them, Mr. Holmes—the Compagnie des Guides, the Ecole de Haute Montagne staff, the instructors of the Ecole de Ski et Alpinisme, the French Army and Air Force. . . . Your friend—Cottier?—is the sixty-eighth climber to die in the French Alps this summer. There will be more. Climbing is a dangerous sport, is it not?"

"It is a sport that some people choose to practice dangerously."

"I see. Do you choose to practice it dangerously?"

"Sometimes."

"Yes. Your marital status?"

"Single. Divorced."

"Single or divorced, Mr. Holmes? One or the other."

"Divorced."

He typed. "Now, the names of your companions were—"
He was interrupted by a heavy rapping on the door.

"*Entrez, entrez,*" he said, nearly shouting.

A short, stocky man of about forty-five entered the room. He wore climbing boots and knickers and moved with that springy, bent-kneed stride that you see on men who spend their lives in the mountains.

Captain Guillot stood up. "This is Robert Holmes," he said. "Holmes—Alain Garnier, one of our guides."

I rose from my chair and we shook hands. The man's palm was callused and lumpy. "What happened?" he asked.

I told him the whole story.

"They are still there, then? On the ledge?"

"Yes."

"What were the conditions of the snow up high?"

"Not too bad this morning, but the slopes will be avalanchy now."

"Yes. And the condition of the rock on the north face?"

"Icy."

"Well, they are not far below the summit. You understand that there may be some difficulty. So many need help now. Perhaps we can obtain use of a helicopter, perhaps not. If not, we will proceed on foot. Most of the professionals are involved on missions at the moment, but many good amateur climbers have volunteered."

"I'll go with you."

"No," he said. "You look very tired."

"But you're short of men."

"Not so short that we must use exhausted climbers. No, rest, Monsieur Holmes. We will rescue the injured man. We will work through the night if conditions permit it. But you understand that we may have to leave the dead man there for a day or two, until all of the living have been saved."

"Of course."

"Ah, this is delicate—the wrong time—but the cost, sir?"

"I'll raise the money," I said.

"Thank you. Of course we would go up there anyway, but there are expenses. . . ."

"I understand. The expenses will be taken care of."

We shook hands again and the guide left the office.

The policeman inserted a fresh sheet of paper into his typewriter. "Now," he said, "the names again, please."

"Etienne Cottier, of Paris."

"Street address and telephone number?"

I gave them.

"He was married?"

"Yes. His wife's name is Daniele. There are two children."

He typed rapidly, made another mistake, erased it and finished the line.

"If you don't mind," I said, "I would like to notify Madame Cottier."

He appeared to be relieved. "Yes, that would be acceptable. It is difficult for a stranger. . . . But be certain

that you do notify her, and soon. Would you like some
more plum brandy?"

"No, thank you."

"Now, this German—Streicher. He is German?"

"Yes. He's from Munich."

"From Munich, you say. I suppose there are many
Streichers living in Munich. Do you possess the address
and telephone number of his family?"

"No. But his passport is at Martigny's. That would con-
tain the address."

"We probably have the information in our hotel reports.
If not, I'll send someone over to Martigny's for the passport and then phone or telegraph his family. Is he married,
do you know?"

"He isn't."

"Well, he must have a mother or a father or a sister or
something somewhere. All right, now would you tell me
exactly how it happened? Slowly, so that I can type along
with you." He tore the sheet from his typewriter and
then inserted a fresh sheet into the machine. "Begin," he
said.

He typed my statement and I signed it.

"That will be all, Mr. Holmes. Thank you. I wish you
further luck in your avoidance of employment. No doubt
you will be terribly relieved when you safely arrive at
retirement age. Good day." And he made a motion with
his hand as if brushing away a bothersome fly.

I left his office, walked down the hallway and through
the big front office and down the steps to the outside. The
sun was hot now. I removed my down jacket and sweater
and stuffed them into the rucksack.

I walked two blocks to a sidewalk café and sat at a

table beneath a sun-faded orange-and-white-striped awning. The waiter brought me a mug of cold beer. Two young American climbers at a nearby table were arguing the dynamic belay. One said that if his leader were falling he'd by God stop the fall *right now,* and to hell with the algebra of rope tensile strength and elasticity and shock loading and all of that. His more scientific friend was in favor of stopping a fall gradually.

A middle-aged Frenchman with a Paris accent was sitting with his wife and two children at the table next to mine. He had a transistor radio, and a portentous voice was intoning, *". . . plus de six morts des alpinistes en Italie, trois Allemands. . . ."*

"Très stupide," the Frenchman said.

I sipped the cold, foamy beer.

The scientific American: "But you use the friction of the rope through the karabiners to help you stop the fall. If you stop the man too quickly you can hurt him or break the rope."

The radio: *". . . quinze morts des Alpes. . . ."*

I lit a cigarette and sipped more beer. I was very tired. Thoughts surfaced and then slipped away again before I could grasp them.

"None of that crap applies with the modern ropes," the unscientific American said, correctly.

". . . dans la face nord de l'Eperon Walker, deux alpinistes en perdition. . . ."

"Très stupide!" the Parisian said.

I finished the beer, picked up my rucksack and left the café.

4

I walked to the main road and hitchhiked a ride west down the valley. The driver wanted to talk about Indochina, but I pretended that I could not speak French and so the ride was silent. I smoked a cigarette and looked out the windows. The Brévent, at 2,526 meters, and its long ridge system were to my right. The Chamonix aiguilles and the Mont Blanc massif were above and to my left. I had to lean far forward in the car seat and twist my neck to see the high snowfields of Mont Blanc. The peak is 15,771 feet high, while Chamonix is only 3,396 feet, a vertical difference of 12,375 feet—over two statute miles.

The *téléférique* to the Aiguille du Midi was operating and the cables gleamed like silken threads in the sunlight. We passed Lac des Gallands and the Ecole d'Escalade. The road crossed the river and the car slowed to pass through Les Bossons. Above the town the Bossons glacier was a great frozen river, poised, a long steep torrent of falls and rapids that had been stopped and silenced by cold. The ice was dirty and littered with rocks at this season. Then we passed the second turnoff to Le Mont and the car picked up speed. I had the driver let me out halfway between Le Mont and Les Houches.

A narrow dirt road twisted off through a checkerboard of fields. I started walking toward the pension. It was very hot now. Puffs of dust exploded at my heels. I could smell the dust and pollen and manure and sun, and it seemed that the odors of the storm lingered in my nostrils too. The rucksack was heavy. The straps bit into my shoulders. Each step required effort. The plum brandy and the beer had relaxed me and I felt separated from myself, as in a dream.

The road bisected the flat valley floor and began tacking up gentle hillsides. It entered a larch forest, winding like a snake, and then gradually petered out into wagon ruts. Another quarter mile and there were some buildings, several acres of cultivated land, a few more acres of fenced pastures, and a creek that was swollen and noisy with glacier melt. A barn with a stone foundation leaned wearily toward the mountains, beginning to surrender in its battle against gravity. The buildings—barn, shed, stable, and a two-story chalet—had been weathered and blackened by eight hundred seasons.

I climbed the split log stairway to the chalet porch and opened the door. Christiane Renaud, Martigny's stepdaughter, was working in the kitchen. She turned and smiled. "Hello!" she said. "You look tired."

"I am."

"You're hungry, too, then."

"No." I drew a glass of water from the kitchen tap and drank it.

"Did the storm interfere with your climb?" she asked.

I turned. I did not know how to tell her. She'd liked Cottier very much, not as a lover but as a friend. He had stayed here for a month every year for six or seven years.

"Well?" she asked.

Christiane was a tall girl in her late twenties with sleek Indian-black hair and gold-flecked eyes and golden skin. Her nose was maybe too Gallic, if one thought that beauty was matching up perfect component features; and her mouth was perhaps too wide if you liked slide rule symmetry. But she was lively and sensual and feminine.

"Where is Etienne?" Christiane asked.

"He's dead."

"Oh, mon Dieu!"

"He was struck by lightning."

"Oh, Jésus, Jésus!"

"I would like to place a telephone call to his wife."

"Oh God, poor Etienne! He was such a laughing man."

I told her the Paris telephone number. She started to cry.

"Write the number down, Christiane."

"What was it? I didn't hear you."

I repeated the number.

She found a pencil and pad of paper in a cabinet drawer and wrote down the telephone number.

"I'll go up to my room now. Ring me when you reach Daniele."

"Poor Madame Cottier. The poor little children. What about the children?"

"Listen to me, Christiane. Get the call through to Paris as soon as possible."

"Yes, yes. Oh, the mountains are wicked!" And she started to cry again.

"Streicher's still in the mountains. He's hurt."

"What do I care about that dirty German!" she cried.

My room was a large, well-lighted rectangle on the second floor. There was a big bed with eiderdown quilts, a writing desk and chair, a dresser, a bedside table with a reading lamp, and a small bathroom. A beamed ceiling slanted from left to right across the room, but there was head space even at the low end.

I got the bottle of Scotch whisky from the dresser, carried it into the bathroom, removed my toothbrush from a glass and poured the glass half full. A splash of water, and then I went to the bed and sat down. I had not turned the faucet off completely and I could hear the spaced dripping of the water. The room smelled of soaps and starches.

I drank some of the whisky and lit a cigarette. Sunlight streamed in through a window and cast a blurry underwater pattern on the hardwood floor.

Hold on, Streicher—"dirty German."

I removed my boots and dropped them to the floor. I unbuckled the straps at my knees and took off my knicker stockings. My feet were greasy to the touch and they smelled vile. I inhaled from the cigarette and returned it to the ashtray. I removed my wool shirt and the top of my long woolen underwear. More whisky, more smoke. The Scotch tasted harsh and sour; the cigarette was making me dizzy. I pulled down my knickers and took off my underwear bottoms. I got a clean pair of shorts from the dresser, put them on and walked over to the wall mirror— three-day growth of beard, dark hollows beneath my eyes, sunburn, dry matted hair.

Really, how stupid this climbing was.

Back to bed and the drink and the cigarette. The cigarette was mostly ash now and so I lit another. I glanced at my wristwatch: 2:33. I rotated the hands until they read 7:00. I would have to get the watch repaired, but until then there was nothing compelling me to wear a memorial around my wrist. Cottier had stopped, not time.

Poor Etienne. Such a laughing man.

The lightning had nearly killed me and Streicher, too. Death was often a matter of inches, of millimeters. Death was a lottery, and once again I had failed to draw the big number. Well, Christ, I was entering the runner-up category pretty regularly.

Right now the rescue party might be en route to retrieve Etienne's body. For a moment I envisioned that it was my body instead: my skin was gray and frozen as hard as stone. My eyes were gelid. My jaws were locked in rictus. The sky had flashed and I'd gone from awareness to nothingness. I was dead. But it didn't work. Empathy cannot follow its object into that *terra incognita*.

The telephone rang. I lifted the receiver. "Hello?"

Daniele came onto the line. "Etienne?" she asked. "Etienne?"

"Daniele, it's Robert Holmes."

There was a long humming silence. She sensed it; she was afraid.

"Etienne," she said.

"He's dead, Daniele."

A long pause. "Who is this?"

"Robert."

"Where are you calling from?"

"Chamonix."

"I know that's not true. Etienne went climbing in Italy."

"We climbed in the Dolomites and then we came here."

"Ah, no."

"Etienne is dead; he was struck by lightning yesterday. I'm sorry."

There was a long silence. "Is he hurt badly?"

"He's dead."

"But no. Not Etienne."

"He was struck by lightning."

"Is he badly hurt?"

"Daniele, for Christ's sake, listen—he is dead."

She began sobbing.

"I'm sorry," I said.

She cried for a time and then she said, "This is so cruel. Why are you telling me these things?"

"It's true," I said.

"You're not Robert. I know Robert's voice."

"Jesus, baby, I really am so sorry."

"Oh, God," she said. "Please tell me this isn't true. Tell me you are both drunk and this is a horribly cruel joke."

"He's dead," I said.

She forced a little laugh. "Robert, let me talk to Etienne now."

"You have to come here," I told her. "The guides are going to recover the body. They'll bring Etienne down late this afternoon or tomorrow sometime. You must be here to decide what to do. Shall Etienne be buried here or in Paris? There are other things. Those decisions must be made by you."

"No, I can't."

"You must."

"It's true, then?"

"Yes."

"What can I tell the boys?"

"Wait to tell them. Come here first, make the arrangements, and when you return home you can talk to the boys."

"I mean—when they are growing up and want to know about their father—what can I tell them?"

"Tell them that he was a good man."

"Is that all?"

"There isn't any more."

"If you aren't killing each other in wars," she said bitterly, "you're killing yourselves climbing mountains or racing cars or . . ." Her voice trailed off and she started crying softly.

"What are you going to do now?"

"I'm going to get someone to stay with the boys and I am going to Chamonix."

"Yes."

"Because Etienne is dead and I must go there."

"Yes. Contact me as soon as you arrive. I'm staying at the Martigny pension north of Chamonix."

"All right."

"Is it clear now?"

"Oh, yes, surely, it is all very clear now. Goodbye, Robert," she said. She broke the connection.

I slept and had one of those perverse, transparent dreams in which one attempts to correct a past mistake. Cottier and I were arguing about continuing a climb. However, it was Etienne who wished to proceed and I who wanted to turn back. It was a useless quarrel, though, since even in the dream Cottier was a dead man.

The room was dark when I awoke. Water still ticked from the bathroom faucet. The luminous hands of the alarm clock glowed eerily in the darkness. It was almost ten o'clock. I felt as if there had been a body exchange during sleep: an old, worn body had replaced my relatively young and healthy one. My muscles ached. My face was sunburned and tautly sore. My lips were sunburned and split. My eyes felt as if they were lubricated with glue. There was a taste in my mouth like wood smoke. I listened to the ticking of the clock and the ticking of water and tried to become familiar with the strange body that now imprisoned my psyche. I had a hint of what it was like to be very old.

I went into the bathroom and took a long hot shower and then shaved. The razor blade was sharp and my skin well lathered, but each stroke felt as if I were drawing broken glass over my face. I had forgotten to use glacier cream yesterday and today. My face was tanned from a summer of climbing, but the sun's reflection off the snow and the ultraviolet rays at high altitudes will burn over and through a tan.

I dressed in a soft white shirt, no tie, gray slacks, dark blue sports jacket and black loafers. The shoes felt very light after I had practically lived in climbing boots for a month.

I took a booster shot of Scotch, turned off the lights and stepped out into the hallway. The house was silent except for the faint droning of an electric motor. Martigny and Christiane had rooms downstairs. Martigny was still up at the refuge. Christiane probably was sleeping. There were four guest rooms on the second floor: mine, the two that had been rented by Cottier and Streicher, and another which was occupied by a man named Pierre Margolin. No light glowed beneath the doors. There was no sound. Margolin was sleeping too, then, or was in town or up in the mountains.

I went down the stairs, passed through the big living room and the kitchen, and went out the back door. It was a soft, hushed night. There was a three-quarter moon, a careless sprinkling of stars, some torn, fibrous clouds. A night bird whistled. I could smell the creek and hear its liquid harmony. I waited until my senses became fully adjusted, until I ceased being an intruder and became a part of the night, and then I walked to the shed and wheeled out my motorcycle. It was a BMW that had cost more than I could afford and went faster than any two-wheeled vehicle should. There was no governor on the machine and none in my mind.

It started on the third attempt. I let the engine warm up for a few minutes and then started down the wagon ruts. Dust gleamed like gold flakes in the conical headlight beam. Trees flashed green and then slid past me into darkness. When I reached the main valley road I turned toward Chamonix and accelerated through the gears. The speedometer needle climbed until it indicated that I was now eligible for several days in jail. Then there was nothing except the wind, cold on my face, and the stuttering roar of the engine, and the center line of the road shooting beneath the front wheel like tracer bullets—and, vaguely perceived, the moon-glinting V-ripples of the river and, ahead, a salting of lights. The speedometer needle bounced off the pin. I heard angels singing.

I slowed to enter Les Bossons and then continued on into Chamonix at a reasonable speed. I parked the bike near a café where I knew the guides often ate and drank. Perhaps I could learn something about the rescue operation there. I dismounted and stood quietly for a moment, until the roar and blur and exhilaration of speed abandoned my senses.

The guide Alain Garnier was sitting alone at a table in the corner of the café. He still wore his climbing clothes and he looked tired. His tan face had been burnished over with new sunburn. The flesh around his eyes was dark. His hair was feathery from the stocking cap. The cap was on the table now, alongside a glass of white wine.

I approached the table. "How did it go?" I asked.

He looked up at me. "Hello," he said. "Would you care to sit down?"

I pulled out a chair. "Can I buy you a glass of wine?" I asked.

"If you have the money and the inclination you can buy me a barrel of wine."

"How long ago did you get down from the mountains?"

"Not more than a half-hour ago."

I signaled the waiter to bring two glasses of the white wine. "Then you got Dieter Streicher down all right?"

"Streicher?" he said. "What Streicher? There was no Streicher."

"What do you mean?"

"The ledge was empty except for the dead man."

"Impossible!"

"Nevertheless...."

"You mean Dieter was gone?"

"I believe that is what I've been saying," he replied dryly.

I could not accept it.

"We recovered the body of the dead man," he said.

"Cottier?"

"If that was the name of the man—yes."

"But listen, it's incredible—what happened to Streicher?"

The guide shrugged. "We managed to obtain a helicopter after a two- or three-hour wait. It took us up to the refuge. The ridge slopes had already avalanched and so we were able to start up immediately. We set up the winch and cable gear at the base of the north snow field. By that time it was dusk, but since we believed there was an injured man on the ledge, I volunteered to go down."

"Did you try to yell down to Streicher first?"

"Of course. We shouted, but there was no reply. We assumed that either he was unconscious or the wind was blowing our voices away. It was very windy up there. So I packed a few medical supplies in my pockets, and the others lowered me and a Stigler-type stretcher. Normally we would have waited until morning. As you can guess, such operations can be quite dangerous in the dark. But I thought at the very least I could go down and give him some food and medication and encouragement. Maybe even stay there on the ledge with him until morning, attend his needs, keep his spirits high."

He paused while the waiter brought us the two glasses of wine.

"Well, it was night by the time I reached the ledge. I found a dead man there, hanging from a piton, but no Streicher."

"But what do you suppose could have happened?"

"I don't know. I've been thinking about it. There was a short length of nylon cord attached to a piton. The cord had been broken or cut. There seem to be two possibilities. This Streicher had a badly broken leg. Perhaps somehow a bone end was pushed through the skin, making a compound fracture. That would account for pain, an enormous pain. Maybe, in his pain and despair, he cut the cord that held him to the mountain and rolled over the side."

"No!" I said. "I firmly splinted his leg. There was no way the break could turn into a compound fracture."

"I disagree. Still, there is another possibility. When the sun came around to the north face it melted the ice and loosened the rock above the ledge. You know that always happens after a thaw. There are rockfalls. Rocks fall down these cliffs all the time, but especially when the sun warms them. So, then, there was a rockfall, perhaps a huge block swept down the face and carried this German away. That would explain the blood and the broken safety cord."

"Did you notice signs of a rockfall?"

"I searched the ledge area thoroughly. There were some deep scars that could have been caused by falling rock."

"Yes, today or ten years ago. Was there any debris on the ledge itself?"

"No. But the momentum of falling rock makes it likely that it would bounce off such a narrow ledge."

"Jesus Christ," I said. I felt sick about it. Cottier was dead; he'd been killed instantly. There had been nothing I could do. But it had seemed certain that Streicher would be saved.

The guide sipped his wine. "Since I was already down there, and since there is nothing that can hurt a dead man, I lashed the body to the stretcher and the others hauled it and me to the top. Your friend's remains do not look very good, though."

"How is that?"

"The ravens got his eyes."

I winced. "That must have happened after Streicher had fallen or been swept away."

"Absolutely. The *choucas* would not have come close to that ledge if there had been a living man there."

"How do you explain the fact that your rockfall carried Streicher away but didn't disturb Cottier's body?"

"What can we do under these circumstances except speculate? How do *you* explain it?"

44

"I can't."

Garnier nodded. "Also, there was a big wind up in the high country. The body—Cottier—was twisted around on the rope so that he faced the rock. The wind moved him and abraded most of the flesh off his face. His face is just raw, thawing ground meat now. Without eyes." He finished his wine in one long swallow.

"Will you have another wine?" I asked him.

"Of course."

I signaled the waiter again.

"God," the guide said, "I'm glad this summer is almost over. Skiers rarely kill themselves, and they tip much better than climbers. Why are climbers such a ragged, poor lot?"

The waiter brought another glass of wine.

I lit a cigarette. I sat quietly for a time and then I said, "Oh, god*damn* it!"

"I understand," he said. "I have lost many friends in the mountains. A brother, too."

"What about the recovery of Streicher's body?" I asked.

"That will have to wait for a few days. There are living still to be helped, and everyone is tired. In three days, four, five, some of the guides will go out and retrieve the German's corpse."

"Where do you think it will be? In the bergschrund?"

"No, farther down the glacier. There have been several falls from the upper section of that wall, and always the body has been found beyond the bergschrund. The glacier is steep and crevassed there at the base of the wall, as you know. The body would hit the ice and then bounce and slide down the slope until it fell into a crevasse or was stopped by a sérac. There is a very big crevasse about a third of the way down the steepest part of the glacier. I would look there first."

"Maybe I'll go out tomorrow or the next day and see if I can locate the body."

"You may find it; you may not. Glaciers have a way of swallowing bodies and not spitting them out for fifty years. Maybe in fifty years this German will arrive at the terminal moraine, nicely frozen, well preserved. But more likely the movement of the ice will grind him up into just a few bone splinters, some hair, and enough leather to make a wallet."

I stared at him.

He smiled thinly. "Sorry." Then he raised his glass. "I must go, but first we should drink a toast to the soul of your dead comrade."

"Comrades," I said.

His eyes slid away from mine and then returned in a defiant stare. "To Monsieur Cottier!" he said.

"And Dieter Streicher!"

He lowered his glass without tasting the wine. "I will risk my own life to save the life of a Streicher—that is my duty. But I won't drink to a Streicher."

"What do you have against Dieter?"

"The son of the devil is half devil."

"What the hell does that mean, Garnier?"

"Dieter Streicher was Adolph Streicher's son," he said. He crumpled his cap in his fist, stood up, nodded at me and walked through the café and out the door.

I crossed a bridge over the river and went to a café called Le Rouge et Blanc. It was an old place built out of logs, with a huge stone fireplace and smoke-blackened ceiling. The floor was pocked from the days when climbers wore nailed boots. On the walls there were signed photographs of climbers from the "golden era": Mummery, Whymper, Croz, Charlet-Straton. The place reeked of one hundred and thirty years of tobacco and wine and lies. The room was crowded now and patrons were loudly telling new lies in five languages.

Ted Fleming, the man I had come here hoping to see, was sitting at a corner table with a pair of lean, long-jawed, sunburned young Englishmen with ugly haircuts. There was an empty chair at their table. I walked over, pulled out the chair and sat down.

"Holmes," Fleming said. "Hello, you bastard. Oh,

Holmes, I am drunk. I'm celebrating. Yes, I believe I am celebrating."

"What are you celebrating, Ted?"

"A promotion. Yes, I'm almost certain that I'm celebrating a promotion."

Fleming worked for a British wire service that had bought some free-lance articles from me during the past year. "Congratulations," I said.

"Here now, we'll have none of that. No envy, Holmes, no vicious and degrading envy. Do you want a job? The head of the French bureau has been booted upstairs and I am now in charge. I'll have to hire someone to fill my position—not my shoes, that's hardly conceivable—and it might as well be you. I'll give you all the choice assignments if you'll learn to suppress that terrible bitter envy of yours. Envy can destroy a man, Holmes. What do you say?"

"It sounds pretty good."

"Sure it does. I'll hire you. Even if you don't know how to use verbs."

"Fuck you."

"But you're learning fast. Buy me a drink now, Holmes, and seal our sacred pact."

"No," I said. "You've had enough and I want to talk to you about something."

"Envious rascal. Oh, sorry, Holmes—this is Ian Burgess and Phil Carter."

I nodded at them.

"Howdy, pard," the man called Ian said.

"Ian talks to Americans that way," Fleming told me.

"I'm just a ridin' and a ropin'. Yep. Nope."

"Don't mind Ian. He wants to be a child when he grows up."

"Theodore," Ian said, "who is this here mean vaga-boose?"

"Ted," I said, "I want to talk to you."

"Well, shut mah mouff," Ian said loudly, working some old and dubious Southern black dialect into his routine.

I turned to him. "I say, old chap. Wizard. Bloody all right. But you know, a little bugger like you actually shouldn't invite a big bugger like me to shut his mouff."

"A sure 'nuff mean vagaboose."

"Fleming," I asked, "can you step outside for a minute?"

"What do you want to hit me for?" Fleming asked.

"Talk. For Christ's sake, Ted, we can't talk in here."

"Don't ever hit your editor. The first rule of journalistic ethics—never hit your editor."

"Come on outside and we'll talk for a minute."

"Sure." But he didn't move.

I grabbed Fleming by the arm and half guided, half dragged him out of the room. When we were outside he slumped back against the building. "Good Lord, all this oxygen—brutal."

"Who is Adolph Streicher?"

"A little punch-up, eh, Holmes?" He moved away from the wall and swung at me. I stepped back and the momentum of his swing carried him forward for a few stumbling steps, and then he fell face down on the gravel. "You got me with a sucker punch," he said. "Do you mind if I get up?"

"No."

"I suppose you'll hit me again when I get up." He slowly

rose to his feet. "I would accept one of your cigarettes except I quit smoking three weeks ago."

I gave him a cigarette and struck a match. He got the tip glowing.

"Ted, please, listen. I'd like you to tell me a few things. You've said that you've been coming to this valley all your life and so probably. . . ."

"More than my life, actually. My parents came here in 1934, when mother was pregnant with me."

"Astonishing. What do you know about a man named Adolph Streicher?"

"Nazi. RSHA. SIPO-SD. *Amt IV*. Bloody monster. Scourge of the Haute-Savoie. One of Brunner's men." He flipped his cigarette away and swung at me again. I ducked, then kicked his legs out from under him; he sprawled on the gravel.

"Ted, sober up for just five minutes."

"Strange," he said in a muffled voice, "how one keeps kissing these same stones over and over again. This stone tastes like the chalk I used to eat in school. But now I wonder *why* I used to eat chalk."

"Get up, Ted. You need some coffee."

"Interesting. When you're a child you taste everything, chalk, coins, worms, carpeting, soil, leaves, blood, feathers, paper, paste, pencil lead, porridge, everything. And then you must rely on those experiences for the rest of your life. How else could you say that something has a chalky flavor or a coppery taste? Now here we have a stone that tastes like charcoal. It *is* charcoal."

"Come on, Fleming."

"Jesus, Holmes, here's one that tastes like dogshit."

I laughed. "How is it that you're familiar with that taste?"

"Porridge. Same flavor."

"All right. Now get up."

"If I do you'll just kick me in the heirs. Been kicking me in the heirs all night long. My heirs will be sickly enough as it is without you putting your toe in. A blood curse, Holmes, I swear it—my dwarf heirs will hunt you down as fast as their little legs will carry them. Here's a stone that tastes like petrol. Cheap, low octane with lots of lead in it."

I bent down, grasped him under the arms, hauled him to his feet and then steadied him.

"Holmes, I'm going to be sick. It was the charcoal, I think. Shouldn't gnaw charcoal on an empty stomach."

I released him and he staggered off into the shadows and vomited. Afterward he was willing to be led to a café where I ordered a big pot of coffee. After one half-hour and four cups of black coffee he seemed about half sober.

"Tell me about Adolph Streicher now."

"Why do you want to know? An article? That's old stuff, and anyway, no one in Europe wants to read about those days."

"Talk."

"All right. In May of 1943 Adolf Eichmann sent a man named Anton Brunner to—"

"I'm interested in Streicher, Ted."

"Look, Holmes, this is a pretty complex business. Let me tell it my way. Or better yet, go away and let me expire in peace."

TOMBS OF BLUE ICE

I lit a cigarette and leaned back in the chair. Fleming would never use one word where ten would do.

"So then. In May of '43 Eichmann sent his special assistant *Hauptsturmfuehrer* Anton Brunner to Paris to take over *Sonderkommando* IV from Dannecker. Are you familiar with the departmentalization of the Nazi security agencies?"

I shook my head.

"Oh, Christ, it's an almost unintelligible bureaucratic maze. There was the *Abwehr*, the military intelligence under Admiral Canaris—until Canaris was arrested and executed. There was RSHA, that is, the *Reichssicherheitshauptamt*, a kind of central ministry of intelligence and counterintelligence. Then we have the elite SD, the *Sicherheitsdienst*, the security service of the chief of the SS—Himmler. The SD had a bureau called SIPO: *Sicherheitspolizei*, or security police. Are you still with me, Holmes?"

"Hell no."

"SIPO was a security branch in the occupied countries. Now, this Anton Brunner was placed in charge of Section IV of SIPO during May of '43, as I said. *Amt* IV was actually a branch of the *Geheime Staatspolizei*. The Gestapo, of course. In this case, *Geheime Feldpolizei*—the secret state police in the field. Clear so far, Holmes?"

"No, but keep going."

"So, Anton Brunner was sent to France because Eichmann believed that France—that is, Dannecker—had been very sluggish in rounding up and deporting the Jews. Brunner was an extraordinarily ruthless bastard, even for a Nazi. And so as the new chief of SIPO-SD IV, it was his job to speed up the program of genocide. But Section IV also decided which gentiles were to be deported to

52

labor camps, arrested, shot as hostages, et cetera, and it controlled a kind of assassination bureau of French citizens called the *Intervention Référat*. And they were also involved in combating terrorists, saboteurs, spies, internal enemies—in other words, the French Resistance."

"Are we going to meet Adolph Streicher soon?"

"Very soon. Patience. Brunner dispatched a team of men to Grenoble. As you probably know, some parts of the Alps were very strong in the Resistance. Adolph Streicher was the number-two man of the Grenoble group, and the Haute-Savoie was his special province."

"And so the people here would have reason to hate Streicher?"

"Hate is hardly the word. Streicher had unlimited power, and he employed it in the usual Nazi style. Terror, torture, the shooting of hostages, the deportation of Jews. The men of these valleys were conscripted for compulsory labor in Germany and many of them never returned. There were irrational arrests, summary executions. People who weren't even born until after the war despise his name."

"Where was he from?"

"Munich. He was a Bavarian, like so many of the Nazis."

"And where is he now?"

"No one knows for sure. Probably dead. Two of his men reported that he'd been killed during the German withdrawal. But you know how those things go. He could be police chief in some little Bavarian village, or living quietly in Spain or Argentina or Paraguay. We might even have seen his face on television during the Olympic broadcasts: one of those plump, middle-aged enthusiastic Bavarians in the crowd."

"What do you think?"

Fleming shrugged. "I have no idea."

"Was there much Resistance activity in this valley?"

"Well, yes, sure. It wasn't as aggressive as, say, the Resistance around Grenoble or Marseilles or Lyon or Limoges, but it existed. Near the end of the war the local Resistance virtually controlled the mountains and the valley, and it forced the German garrison to surrender. But listen, the French Resistance is highly overrated."

"Some of them did a good job."

"Sure, and so did the undergrounds in Italy and Poland and Greece and Yugoslavia and Czechoslovakia and Norway and Holland and elsewhere. But all you hear about are the French. The French are even better promoters than you Americans, except while you sell soaps and refrigerators, the French sell France."

"Ted, do you know Jules Martigny?"

"Yes."

"Was he in the local Resistance?"

"He was, yes."

"Who was he with? The *Armée Secrète*? *Franc Tireurs et Partisans*? Some other group?"

"The F.T.P., I believe."

"Is he a Communist?"

"I don't know. But listen, many French who weren't the slightest bit red fought with Communist Resistance groups. They were the toughest and best disciplined and most effective."

"Do you know Alain Garnier?"

"Oh, Holmes, I have such a bloody awful headache and I'm going to puke up a gallon of coffee. Can't this wait?"

"No."

"Garnier—what do you want to know?"

"Was he in the Chamonix valley Resistance?"

"Yes. But I don't know who he was with."

"Was this Adolph Streicher responsible for the death of any member of Garnier's family?"

"I heard something—I believe his two sons were drafted into the compulsory labor program and never returned from Germany."

"And Martigny?"

"Martigny's fifteen-year-old son was shot as a hostage."

"By Streicher?"

"Well, Streicher didn't pull the trigger. But he selected the hostages."

"And so both Martigny and Garnier would have good reason to hate Streicher."

"Well, sure. What is all this about, Holmes?"

"Do you know Christiane Renaud?"

"A lovely girl."

"What happened to her father? Was he in the Resistance?"

"Yes, but not in a combat role. He was a farmer who provided food and sometimes shelter to the fighters. He was arrested in a raid, taken to Grenoble and later shot. In fact, I think he was shot at the same time as Martigny's son. Martigny adopted the girl after the war was over."

"Now, listen, did Adolph Streicher have a son?"

"I have no idea."

"Ted, I suppose you heard about the accident."

"What accident?"

"Cottier was killed by lightning yesterday."

"Etienne? No! Oh, Jesus. Goddamn it, Holmes."

"We were climbing with a young man from Munich named Dieter Streicher. Alain Garnier claims that Dieter

was the son of Adolph Streicher. Dieter's leg was broken.
I left him on a ledge with his leg well splinted, with plenty
of food and water, and securely pinned to the mountain.
Garnier claims that when he went down to the ledge early
this evening the man was gone. He said there was blood
on the rock and the anchor cord was broken and Dieter
was simply not there."

"Well, Jesus . . . tell me about it."

I told him the whole story, beginning with the storm and
ending with my conversation with Garnier an hour earlier.

"Holmes," Fleming said when I had finished, "you don't
really think that Alain Garnier killed young Streicher, do
you?"

"Garnier or Martigny. Martigny had sufficient time to go
up from the refuge, kill Dieter and then return. It's
possible."

"Sure, it's possible. When I was twelve years old our
vicar, a married man with four children, ran off with a
homosexual circus acrobat. Ever since then I've known
that anything is possible."

"Except," I said, "Dieter Streicher was innocent of his
father's crimes. He couldn't have been more than one or
two years old in 1943."

"Don't be naive. The sins of the fathers *are* often visited
upon the sons. What does innocence have to do with it?
Most of Adolph Streicher's victims were innocent too."

"Ted, I just can't believe that Dieter committed suicide
or was swept away by an avalanche or rockfall."

"All right. Let's assume that there has been a murder.
You have two suspects, Garnier and Martigny, both of
whom would have the opportunity and motive, although it

seems that Martigny would have been awfully short of
time."

"No. Martigny probably had several hours before the
rescue party arrived."

"Fine. You have two suspects. Now what?"

"I'll try to prove that Dieter was killed."

"Sure he was killed; he fell two thousand feet. Now find
a pathologist who can establish evidence of violence on a
corpse that has fallen two thousand feet."

"Tuesday morning I'm going to try to find Dieter's body.
Do you want to come along?"

"I can't. I have to go to Paris tomorrow. But phone me
if you learn anything."

"Am I on the payroll?"

"Starting tomorrow. But listen, don't let this business
drag on. I doubt if you'll learn anything, though it would
make a hell of a story if you did—pastoral mountain
setting, Nazi criminals, Resistance fighters, fathers and
sons, blood vendetta, revenge across the decades, all of
that. Give it a few days and then come to Paris."

"Good enough."

"Nothing will come of this."

"Probably not."

"But see what you can dig up."

"I will, I will."

7

I remained at the pension all day Monday waiting for Daniele Cottier to telephone. During the morning I washed a few items and hung them in the bathroom to dry. I rubbed linseed oil into the wooden shaft of my ice axe. I carefully examined the climbing rope for cuts and abrasions and then recoiled it. I cleaned my boots and sprayed them with silicone waterproofing.

At eleven o'clock I put away my gear, lit a cigarette and walked to the window. Christiane was outside in the yard, hanging some clothes on a wire that stretched from a corner of the shed to a tree.

Apparently she intended to sunbathe too. She wore a bikini, and nearby, in a splash of sunlight, a blanket was spread out over the grass. I watched her as she stretched to pin a blouse on the wire. Christiane usually dressed carelessly, and in clothing she appeared slender, almost thin. But now I could see that she was a bigger girl than I had supposed. Her legs were long and smooth and looked strong. The bikini revealed her narrow waist and the heavy female curve of her hips. When she leaned down over the wicker basket I saw that she was heavy breasted too. Her oiled skin gleamed in the sunlight. Her black hair shone with silvery highlights. She moved gracefully up and down the line, bending, stretching, reaching. To me, celibate for almost two months, it seemed a kind of erotic ballet.

And then she sensed something. She suddenly turned and looked directly up at my window. I smiled. She said something. I could hear her voice but could not distinguish the words. Her mouth formed into a pout.

I pulled up the window and leaned over the sill. "You look marvelous in a bikini," I called.

"You are a sneak!" she cried.

"You're lovely."

She laughed. "A nice sneak, it seems to me."

"If you'll come up to my room I'll rub some more suntan oil on your body."

"That sounds interesting." She shaded her eyes with a palm. Her other hand was on her hip.

"Will you?"

"Will I what?"

"Come up here."

"And then what?"

"I'll rub you with suntan oil."

"And then what?"

"I'll make love to you."

"And then what?"

I couldn't think of what happened next.

60

She laughed.

"Come up here or I'll slash my wrists."

"I really don't care much for this long-range seduction."

"I'm trying to close the range."

"And so I drop everything and run up the stairs to your room and jump into bed. Like that. And you, Monsieur, must do nothing but lean out the window and call to me. That would save energy and possibly preserve your little potency, but I don't care for the technique."

"I just remembered what we'll do afterward."

"And what is that?"

"We'll go into Chamonix and have an excellent dinner at the best restaurant in town. Fine wine, candlelight, string music. . . ."

"Reverse procedure, eh? First the love and then the dinner. But I'm sure it would turn out to be last week's soup and yesterday's wine in some climbers' café." She turned and walked over to the clothes basket.

I watched her for a moment and then I went down the stairs and outside.

It was a sunny day that smelled of grass and resin and heated earth. Tree leaves spun and cracked in the warm breeze. Christiane was lying face down on the blanket now. I crossed the yard and knelt beside her. "You think I'm worth descending all those stairs for?" she asked without moving or opening her eyes.

I leaned down and kissed her on the shoulder.

"How does the suntan lotion taste?"

"Like cloves and cinnamon."

"Really?"

"No, it tastes awful."

She turned over onto her back and looked at me. "Stop hovering over me like a vulture."

I smiled and sat back on the grass. "Is Jules still in the mountains?"

"Yes. He should be down this afternoon. There will be no guardian at that refuge for the rest of the season."

"Where is Pierre Margolin?"

"I believe he is in the mountains too."

"Does Pierre climb?"

"Not really. Only as much as is necessary to study the plants and flowers. He's a botanist, you know."

"Yes. I don't suppose he goes very high, then."

"There aren't an awful lot of plants in the high mountains, are there?"

"Not too many. How long has he been gone?"

"Three days."

"Perhaps he's in trouble because of the storm."

"Do you think he might be collecting pine cones on the West Face of the Aiguille du Dru?" she asked, smiling. "Or picking glacier orchids on Mont Maudit?"

"Not very likely, is it?"

"No."

"Do you climb, Christiane?"

"Not as much as I'd like. There is too much work around here. Next summer I am going to insist that Jules hire a full-time helper."

"Perhaps you'll be able to do a little climbing this autumn."

"Perhaps."

"Would you care to climb with me?"

She looked at me quietly for a moment. "That would be all right."

62

"How good are you?"

"I have led fifth-degree climbs and followed on sixth-degree."

"You're very good, then."

"For a woman?"

"No, just good. Shall we try the Jardin Ridge of the Aiguille Verte?"

"Yes." She hesitated. "And then let's do the South Face of the Dent du Géant. I've never done that."

"It's a fairly difficult climb and you're not in training."

"Can you lead it?"

"Yes."

"I can climb it as a second, even now. Shall we go tomorrow? Jules will be here then and he can operate the pension. I really am so sick of being a prisoner in this valley. I must get away to the mountains or to Paris or *somewhere*. Shall we go climbing together tomorrow, then?"

"Tomorrow I'm going out and search for Dieter Streicher's body," I said.

"Oh."

"We'll go climbing together in a few days."

"Yes."

"Christiane, did you know all along that Dieter Streicher was the son of Adolph Streicher?"

"Yes," she said quietly, looking at me.

"I heard that Dieter's father was responsible for the death of your father and Jules's son."

"And others," she said.

"Did you hate Dieter?"

"No."

"What you said yesterday. . . ."

"I didn't hate him, really. But I couldn't like him, either. Do you understand?"

"I think so."

"Why did he come here? Here, of all the places in the world? To *this* valley, *this* house!"

"I don't know. He was a climber. Maybe because Chamonix has the finest climbing in the Alps."

"Is that why?"

"And he was innocent of his father's crimes."

"Yes, all right. Yes. But simple taste, simple discretion . . . ordinary sensitivity. These stupid Teutons. They have the sensitivity of granite. If *your* father were a murderer, would you sit down at a table and eat and drink with the families of his victims?"

"No," I said, "but maybe that's exactly what Dieter wanted to do."

"But why?"

"I don't know, Christiane. It could be very complex. Perhaps he came here because he did feel terribly guilty for what his father had done."

"Does that make sense?"

"It could. Maybe he was hoping to demonstrate to himself and to you that he was different, that he was innocent."

"He humiliated us with his presence because he was ashamed and sorry and guilty?"

"Possibly. Why didn't you send him away?"

"I don't know," she said tiredly. "I really don't know. Maybe it was as you say. It might have been. . . . Listen, I am sorry he is dead. He seemed nice enough in that clumsy German way. I am sorry that he is dead, but a part of me is glad, too. Delighted, even. That's the way it is. That's the way I am. The son of Adolph Streicher is dead. How sad. How beautiful."

"Christiane, do you know Alain Garnier the guide?"

"Of course."

"Was Adolph Streicher responsible for the death of anyone close to him?"

"Alain's two sons were conscripted for labor in Germany. They were among the more than two hundred thousand Frenchmen who did not return after the war."

"Is Alain Garnier bitter over the loss of his sons?"

"Well, certainly. Listen—have you finished with your rude questioning?"

"If you think it's time I finished."

"I do think so."

"I'd like to pan the gold dust from your eyes," I said.

"You're a little strange," she said.

"You smell of exotic tropical musks."

"The suntan lotion," she said, smiling. And then she said, "Wait." She sat up and turned her head slightly. "The telephone is ringing in the house."

"I don't hear anything."

"It's ringing."

"It may be Daniele Cottier," I said. I got up and ran across the yard and entered the house and ran up the stairs to my room. I lifted the receiver. "Hello," I said.

"Robert?"

"Daniele, where are you?"

"In Chamonix."

"I'll meet you there in twenty minutes. Where will you be?"

"They took me to see Etienne," she said. Her voice was flat.

65

"They shouldn't have."

"It was necessary."

"Where are you calling from?"

"His face was almost gone," she said. "His face, his eyes. . . ."

"Where are you now, Daniele?"

"I'm returning to Paris this afternoon. Etienne will be shipped there on the train."

"Daniele, I want to see you."

"No."

"I want to talk with you."

"No," she said. "I don't care to see any of his friends."

I said nothing.

"Not ever again. Etienne is dead. That life is gone. Do you understand?"

"No."

"I don't want to see you, Robert, or any of his mountain friends."

"All right. When will the funeral be? And where in Paris?"

"I don't want you there, either."

"I'm going to attend the funeral, Daniele. Etienne was my friend."

"Please," she said. "Please don't come. Can't you understand? I don't want to see you, Robert, not ever again."

I hesitated. "Do you blame me for his death?"

"No. No, I just blame his wildness. He had a wife and two children and still he was wild. He risked his life in the mountains while we stayed home, and it never even occurred to him to buy insurance for us. He gambled with all our lives. He was wild and now he's dead and all he left us was debts. And I don't want to know the people who

66

shared his cruel wildness. You're wild, too, Robert. I only want to know tame, dull, ordinary people. I myself want a life that is tame and dull and ordinary. And now do you finally understand?"

"I'm beginning to," I said.

"The air is too thin and cold where you and Etienne and the others live."

"All right, Daniele, your point is clear now. What about Etienne's possessions here at the pension?"

"Is there anything of value?"

"Just some clothing and a little climbing gear."

"You keep it all, Robert."

"I guess that's it, then."

"That is it."

"Well, I hope none of your tame, dull, ordinary new friends get hit by a bus or develop cancer. Christ knows what an injustice it is when tame, dull, ordinary people have to die."

"I'm sorry, Robert," she said. "Goodbye."

"Goodbye, Daniele."

The door to Cottier's room was unlocked. I went inside and began gathering up all of his things. He had taken some of his mountain gear on the climb, of course, but there was still quite a lot remaining in the room: pitons, karabiners, chock nuts, a bolt kit, *étriers,* a brand new coil of Perlon rope, lightweight rock-climbing shoes, a down sleeping bag, a bivouac tent, odds and ends. It all made a big mound in the center of the floor. Then I went through the drawers and closet: a suit, underwear and socks, two pairs of slacks, a sweater, several shirts, a shaving kit, a photo of Daniele and the children in a cheap cardboard frame. It was a depressing business.

It is true that when a man dies his possessions seem to lose life with him. They cease being useful objects and become abstractions. They somehow become absurd, al-

most comical in their gratuitousness. I didn't understand
it, but it was subjectively true. I decided to mail the photograph to Daniele and give away the rest of his things.

I carried everything to my room and stashed it away in
the closet. I splashed a little whisky into a glass and sat
down on the edge of the bed. I felt as tired as if I'd soloed
a difficult climb. Well goddamn it. Etienne was the third
man who had died while climbing with me. The fourth if
I wanted to count Dieter Streicher, which I did not. A
skull smashed by a falling rock; a snow avalanche; and
now lightning. I tried to remember their faces and failed.
I could not even recall how Etienne had looked. All I saw
was an eyeless face that had been abraded to pulp. Etienne
was literally faceless now. The others were faceless in my
memory. That was as good a metaphor of death as any
other.

I slept for a time and was awakened by a persistent
tapping. The light had changed in my room. Dusk was not
more than an hour away. The light four-beat tapping on
my door continued. I got out of bed, crossed the room and
opened the door. A middle-aged man of about my height,
but heavier, stood in the doorway. He had lashless blue
eyes, bristly gray hair, jaws and mouth under great tension,
like a closed trap, and very erect posture. It looked as
though his spine had fused together into a solid rod. There
was a resemblance to Dieter Streicher around the mouth
and eyes.

"Yes?" I asked.

He offered me his hand. "Mr. Holmes?"

"Yes."

"I am Walter Streicher."

I clasped his hand. It was a big hand but the grip was
brief and gentle. "Come in," I said.

He passed by me into the room and I closed the door. "Would you like something to drink?" I asked. "I have some whisky."

"No, thank you." His voice was evenly modulated and he spoke English with a noticeable glottal quality.

"Sit down."

"Thank you." He walked over to the desk chair and sat down, breaking only at the knees. He sat there stiffly. "Dieter Streicher was my nephew," he said. "His mother received a telegram from the Chamonix police Sunday afternoon saying that her son had been injured in a climbing accident. Another telegram arrived very late Sunday night informing her that Dieter was dead. She is distraught, of course, and I've come in her place to attend to the necessary details."

I nodded.

"Mademoiselle Renaud has told me that you were with Dieter at the time of the accident."

"That's right."

"How was he killed?"

"I don't know."

"But you were with him."

"I was with him at the time of the accident. He had been burned by lightning and his leg was broken, but other than that he was all right when I left him Sunday morning."

"Please," he said. "Explain."

"Are you sure you won't have a drink?"

"No. Well, yes, perhaps I would. I have some very good cognac in Dieter's room—I am staying there tonight. Would you mind if I went for it?"

"Of course not."

"Will you have a glass?"

"I believe I will."

He left the room and a moment later returned with a bottle of Cordon Bleu and two glasses. "Shall I pour?" he asked.

"Go ahead."

He carried the bottle and glasses to the desk. I watched him. He was slow and precise in all of his actions; each movement apparently required study in order that it be correctly performed. A thoughtful pause separated each distinct act: align the glasses on the desk top, pause, remove the cork from the bottle and set it aside, pause, carefully measure out equal portions of the cognac, pause, retrieve the cork and place it firmly in the bottle, pause, shift the bottle where it will not be accidentally knocked to the floor, pause once again to see that everything is safe and symmetrical, then pick up the two glasses. . . . He poured drinks with all the caution of a demolitions expert defusing a bomb.

He handed me a glass and then returned to the desk chair. "Please, I don't understand. What happened to my nephew?"

I told him the story. I gave him the hard facts only. I did not speculate.

He sat quietly for a time and then asked, "And Dieter was well when you left him Sunday morning?"

"He had a broken leg. And he had been burned by lightning."

"Yes, but otherwise?"

I shrugged. "He was a strong, healthy young man. I really wasn't worried about his condition when I left. He might have gone into shock, of course."

"But that would not account for his disappearance."

"That's right, it wouldn't."

"And this guide—Garnier—he believes that Dieter either killed himself or was swept away by a rockfall?"

"Yes."

"Dieter would not have killed himself," he said.

"I don't think so either."

"Then you also believe it was a rockfall?"

I shrugged.

He looked steadily at me, perhaps thinking, as I had, that it didn't quite add up. He got up and walked to the window and stood there for a time, looking down into the yard.

"A beautiful valley," he said finally.

I did not reply.

"My brother spent some time in the French Alps during the war years."

"I know."

He turned and faced me. "Mademoiselle Renaud told me that you intend to search for Dieter's body tomorrow."

"That's right. It will probably be a few days before the guides can get around to recovering the body. I thought I would go out and try to locate it."

"May I come with you?"

"I don't think that would be a good idea."

"I'm very fit," he said.

"Do you climb?"

"No, but I do a great deal of hiking, some of it in mountainous terrain."

"Hiking and glacier travel are different things."

"Will there be any technical difficulty?"

"A little."

"You could teach me the little I would need to know, then."

"That would slow me down considerably."

"But isn't it dangerous to travel alone on a glacier?"

"It can be."

"Alone, you would have to proceed slowly and cautiously. With another man, using a rope for safety . . ."

I thought about it. "Let's do it this way," I said. "You come with me in the morning. During the hike in I'll judge whether or not you're competent to continue. You must agree that if at any time tomorrow I tell you to return to the valley, you will do so without argument."

"Agreed," he said.

"You'll need some gear."

"What?"

"A good pair of boots, crampons, an ice axe, warm clothing. Buy wool clothing. Long underwear, shirt, sweater, stockings, heavy wool trousers or knickers. A down jacket, a waterproof poncho. And a down sleeping bag—we'll be staying out overnight."

"Anything else?"

"Yes. A good-sized rucksack. Dark glasses or goggles. A small Primus stove and fuel. And food—buy some food."

He nodded. There was a hinge in his upper spine after all. "I'll go into Chamonix immediately and buy everything you've said."

"Buy the clothing and food, and rent everything else."

"What time do you intend to leave tomorrow?"

"Sometime around noon."

"So late?"

"Dieter won't become impatient. We'll hike up the glacier tomorrow afternoon, bivouac, and then conduct the search the day after."

"As you say."

I walked him to the door.

"Thank you," he said, putting his hand on the doorknob.

"You're welcome. Just remember our agreement."

"Certainly." He paused. "Perhaps I'll look up this guide Garnier while I'm in Chamonix."

"He may be in the mountains."

He hesitated. Close up, his eyes appeared less blue: they were small and grayish blue and rimmed by red, puffy, lashless lids. It looked as though there were a sty on each of his eyelids. "Dieter—what kind of a boy was he?"

"He was your nephew. You lived in the same city."

"We were close when he was a child," Streicher said. "After the war. But when he became a man he traveled a lot. And there was conflict between us. Dieter did not care for my generation of Germans."

"A lot of people don't."

He smiled. It was the first time he'd shown his teeth: they were small and crooked and gray. "Including yourself?"

I shrugged. "You were not an admirable people in those days."

"Do you believe in collective guilt, Mr. Holmes?"

"I'm not certain. Sometimes yes, sometimes no."

"My brother was a war criminal," he said.

I nodded.

"I was not. Do I share my brother's guilt?"

"I don't know, Streicher. That seems to me something that you alone have to work out."

He smiled again, a dismal smile that soured at the corners.

"I served in the Luftwaffe for six years, and during all of that time I killed no one."

"I'm not judging you, Streicher. Let's drop the subject."

"I harmed no one."

"If you insist. What were your duties then?"

"I was an aircraft mechanic, an officer, in command of a large ground crew."

"A pacifist might claim that you were as guilty as the pilots or bombardiers for any deaths that resulted from your work."

"Are you a pacifist, Mr. Holmes? Are the American people?"

"No. If we were I might have gone through college singing the Horst Wessel song at fraternity beer parties."

"May we get one thing straight, Mr. Holmes?"

"If we must."

"In the interest of harmony. . . . There are very few people on this planet who despise the Nazis more than I. Very, very few. I believe you had to suffer under that regime in order to hate it properly."

"Streicher, listen—you brought up the subject and it is you who've pursued it. I'm not judging you. And now don't forget your cognac."

"Keep it. I'll buy another. We Germans are still plundering Europe, but this time with marks instead of Mausers." Again his smile faded sourly at the corners.

"You'd better go into Chamonix before the shops close."

"Yes. Thank you. I'll be ready tomorrow."

"Just don't wear your hair shirt."

He left then, finally.

At seven o'clock I went downstairs for dinner. Martigny and Christiane were in the kitchen. They were quarreling and they paused only briefly, long enough to stare at me blankly, and then they resumed the fight. They spoke rapidly in the Haute-Savoie dialect, and I could not understand all of what they said. But they were arguing about

Walter Streicher. Martigny stood in the center of the room, feet spread, mutilated hands gesturing, face darkened with blood. His voice was a monotone: a single, throbbing low note. It was not a shout, but it hammered in a way that tore at the nerves more than any shout. Martigny said that he would not sit at his table with the man. He had submitted before and had eaten with another Streicher, but he would not give in now, not with this one. He would not, he could not. Why had Christiane taken him into the chalet? How could she? How could she cook and serve food to that man and then sit down and eat with him? That was a kind of cannibalism: it was like eating the flesh of her father and his, Martigny's, son. The man was Adolph Streicher! *Adolph Streicher.* He repeated the name six or seven times with metronomic timing. Adolph Streicher.

Christiane was defensive at first, and then she began to cry. But suddenly she revolted and started screaming at her stepfather. I could understand almost nothing of what she said. She screamed abuse, though—the voice and gestures often tell more than the words can convey. She said she was sick of his tyranny. She was leaving. Yes, by God, she was leaving!

Martigny slowly raised his hands. His face had not changed. He stood there, a squat, powerful, ugly bear, and raised his mutilated hands and cupped them as if holding a ball above his head. Despite her rage, Christiane became silent. And then slowly, still in the hammering monotone, Martigny said, "If he is at this table tomorrow night, I will kill him. With these hands I will kill him and then hang him from a meat hook in the barn."

Christiane was not wholly intimidated. "And will you kill me too?"

Martigny stared at her for a long time. He lowered his

hands. And then surprisingly, pathetically, he began to weep. "Ah, no, Christiane," he said, sobbing like a child. He covered his face with hands that looked like eagle talons. He wept. "You are like my daughter," he said. "I love you."

"Your love is destroying me," she said fiercely.

It seemed to me that there was something subtly incestuous about this exchange even though they were not related by blood, and even though I was absolutely certain that there had never been and never could be anything overtly sexual between them. But they were mutually enslaved by a confusion of loves. And I sensed that at some moment in the past the originally enslaved, Christiane, had become more master than subject. The emotional chains were exactly the same, but there had been a shift in dominance. Martigny, so strong physically, was the weaker in this more delicate and devious sort of struggle.

Martigny abruptly turned and went through the door. We heard his footsteps on the stairs, and then it was silent. Christiane, exhausted, sat down at the table and rested her face in her palms. She remained this way for some time, then she lifted her head and looked at me.

"You," she said contemptuously. "You did not even have the courtesy to leave the room while we quarreled."

"I should have," I said. "I'm sorry."

"I despise you for that."

"I'm sorry," I said again.

"I hate you."

"I know I should have left," I said, irritated now, "but it was like watching a cobra and a mongoose—fascinating and deadly."

"Do you enjoy that?"

"No, but I can't help watching."

"Do you always enjoy being the observer, the outsider?"

"There are advantages."

"The problem, *Monsieur Americain,* is that if you cannot be touched, then there is no way you can ever touch another."

"The thing I hate most," I said, "is receiving lectures from unhappy people. No happy person has ever advised me. There must be some sort of unofficial quarantine between the happy and unhappy."

"And which are you, *Monsieur Americain?*"

"I'm a tourist in both countries."

"And a citizen of neither."

"That's right. I think the soup is boiling."

She got up and left the room.

There were already cheese and sausage and fruit and two bottles of wine on the table. I turned off the burner beneath the soup, spooned some into a bowl and went to my chair.

A few minutes later Streicher came in with a full rucksack and some packages. He carried everything up to his room and then returned.

9

Streicher and I had almost finished eating when the door opened and Pierre Margolin entered the room. He was dressed in rough woolens and carried an enormous rucksack. "Bonjour, bonjour," he said in a deep, resonant voice. He swung the rucksack awkwardly off his shoulders and placed it in the corner. Margolin did not look natural in outdoor clothing; he seemed to belong in the conservatively cut dark business suits he usually wore. I did not know him well, but he impressed me as basically an urban man, bourgeois, one of Daniele's good and tame and ordinary people. Only a tart sense of irony kept him from appearing pompous.

He was in his middle forties, short and plump, bald except for a crescent of hair above each ear and a few strands slicked obliquely over the top of his head. A round face, small eyes behind thick glasses, an air of cheerful mediocrity. That was how I saw him at the moment.

"Monsieur Holmes," he said to me, "I heard; I am sorry. Etienne. Madame Cottier, her children. . . . '*Maintenant, les petits sommeillent tristement . . .*' "

Streicher lifted his head. " '*Vous diriez, a les voir, qu'ils pleurent dormant.*' "

"Ah, you know Rimbaud, Monsieur. Your accent is terrible, but still, you know *The Orphans' Gift*. '*Les touts petits enfants ont le coeur sensible!*' "

"Pierre," I said, "this is Walter Streicher. Streicher— Pierre Margolin. Pierre is a botanist who specializes in alpine flora."

Streicher rose and offered his hand, but at the same instant Margolin pivoted and began drawing a glass of water from the tap. "Enchanted," Margolin said, his back turned.

Streicher stood quietly for a moment and then slowly settled back into his chair.

"Pierre," I said, "there is still plenty of food left."

He finished his glass of water and then turned. "I've eaten," he said. "But perhaps a piece of cheese. Or one of those cucumbers." He walked around the table and sat across from Streicher. He glanced around the table and then speared some cucumber slices with a fork and released them onto his plate.

"Streicher," he said. "You must be related to the unfortunate lad who stayed here until recently."

"He was my nephew."

"Ah, yes. And are you possibly related to Julius Streicher, the late Nazi *Gauleiter* of Nuremberg?"

"No."

Margolin salted his cucumber slices. "Perhaps you are related to Horst Streicher of the *Schutzstaffel*? He was involved in the Polish purification program, you may remember."

"No," Streicher said, staring levelly at Margolin.

"*Obergruppenfuehrer* Wolf von Streicher of the Waffen-SS?"

"No," Streicher said.

I watched them.

"Hans Peter Streicher of Dachau notoriety?"

"No."

Now Margolin looked up. "Adolph Streicher, then?"

"He was my brother."

Margolin smiled. "I know," he said. "You look exactly as he would look today. But that isn't surprising."

"Did you know my brother?"

"No, but I have studied photographs of him."

"Why have you studied his photographs?"

Margolin casually rolled up his sleeve and revealed a tattoo. "I am an alumnus of several concentration camps. Mauthausen was the last."

"Did my brother send you there?"

"Well, it's difficult—"

"Did he?"

"I have never really determined who sent me to the camps. Sometimes I think it was your brother. Or was it Hitler? Himmler, Eichmann, Brunner? The French lady who denounced me and my family to the Gestapo? The Gestapo team who arrested us? Three of the four were Frenchmen, like myself. The guards at the Drancy camp? The SS detachment which escorted us to Poland? I don't know. But occasionally I wake up in the middle of the night believing that it was the whole world that sent me to the camps. But that is paranoid. What do you think, Herr Streicher?"

"I think there is nothing I can say."

"There really isn't. Were you a Party member?"

"No."

"What?"

"Luftwaffe."

"Where?"

"Germany and France."

"Did you belong to any organizations determined illegal by the Allies?"

"What is the purpose of this inquisition?"

"You don't have to answer."

"I realize that. I do not have to justify myself to you."

"Of course not."

"I was an aircraft mechanic."

"You do not have to explain, Herr Streicher."

"You are making accusations."

"No, I am not. But even if I were, you would not have to defend yourself."

"I am not like my brother!"

"I believe you."

"He became a beast, a criminal!"

"Please, please, calm yourself. It's all right. I understand perfectly. You have no need to convince me of your innocence."

"He was a murderer!"

"Oh, he was worse than that," Margolin said.

I watched them. Margolin was gently destroying all of my conceptions of him.

84

"But his crimes aren't mine," Streicher said. "I'm not responsible for what he did."

"Certainly not."

Streicher turned to me in appeal. His composure was gone. He looked bewildered, afraid. I said nothing, and so he turned back to Margolin.

"Why are you doing this to me?"

Margolin raised his eyebrows. "What? What am I doing?"

"You have no right to interrogate me this way."

"I'm not interrogating you at all, Herr Streicher."

"I refuse to answer any more questions."

"That is your choice."

"I've never harmed you or your people."

"You were just a simple aircraft mechanic."

"I lost in the war, too. I lost my wife and son."

"Everyone lost. There were no winners."

"My wife and my son were killed in an American air raid." He glanced accusingly at me and then turned back to Margolin. He was very agitated and sweating now. And the more excited he became, the calmer Margolin was.

"And what was your wife's name?" Margolin asked sympathetically.

"Hilda. Her name was Hilda."

"And your son?"

"Walter. We named him Walter, after me, and after my father too. Both my father and I were named Walter."

"Did you have any pet names for your son?"

"No."

"You didn't?"

"No—yes. I sometimes called him *Panzerfaust*."

"That's right," Margolin said. "And the poor child had a bone disease."

"Rickets. He had rickets—the wartime diet."

"Yes. And on your last visit home before the air raid that killed them, you brought little *Panzerfaust* a present."

Streicher paused. "How did you know?"

"What was the present?"

"A toy."

"What kind of toy?"

"It was a toy Messerschmitt 109."

"That's correct."

"But how do you know?"

"The toy airplane was found in your son's hands when the collapsed building was excavated."

"But how do you know all of this?"

"We've made inquiries."

"But *why?*"

"Well . . . you might really be Adolph."

"What? No. No, Adolph is dead."

"Perhaps."

"No, he is!" Streicher picked up a wine glass with his right hand and held it with the tips of his fingers and thumb. He gently rolled the glass and then set it down in front of Margolin. "Take that."

Margolin smiled. "As you certainly know, identical twins have identical fingerprints."

"But I am *Walter* Streicher!"

"What armament did the ME 109s carry?"

"Two 20-millimeter cannons and two 7.9-millimeter machine guns."

"That's correct. Who made the engines?"

"Daimler-Benz."

"They didn't have fuel injection. Why not?"

"But they did have a fuel injection system. They were not affected by negative G, like the British Hurricanes."

"Where were the ME 109s and ME 110s fabricated?"

"In Leipzig and Augsburg. And later in Wiener Neustadt."

"Where were you trained?"

"In Austria."

"Where?"

"No!" Streicher said, nearly shouting. "No, listen—I am sick of this! I do not have to answer your questions."

"Certainly not. But surely it is a simple thing—"

"No more!"

"All right. But maybe you will just tell me—"

"Nothing!" Streicher said. He rose swiftly to his feet. "I am a man," he said. "I am entitled to a little dignity. No, no more. You have no right." He left the kitchen, and we heard the sound of his footsteps receding as he climbed the stairs rapidly toward his room.

Margolin and I sat in silence for some time. Then I said, "Did you learn what you wanted to?"

He shrugged. "I think he is probably Walter Streicher, as he claims."

"He seemed to know something about the aircraft of those days."

"An afternoon's study. I didn't judge him by his technical knowledge, but by his bearing, his being."

"You opened him up pretty quickly."

"It's a matter of knowing what strings to pluck."

"And what strings did you pluck, Pierre?"

"Guilt."

"Then you believe he's guilty?"

"No, I think, I *think* he's innocent. He reacted with enormous guilt. The innocent often do, the guilty almost never. Adolph Streicher could have faced me without guilt, with contempt even. I'm a Jew, after all. Adolph Streicher might have been frightened, but not guilty. No, the only way you can reach the Adolph Streichers is by terrorizing them. They're vulnerable to terror because they've exercised it. They know how brutal one man can be to another because they've committed the maximum brutality."

"But Adolph Streicher might have changed in all these years. He might feel guilty for his crimes now."

Margolin smiled. "Do you think so?"

"Do you?"

"No."

I lit a cigarette. "No one has told me that Adolph Streicher had a twin brother."

"No one around here would know it."

"Today, Martigny called him Adolph. He believed the man was Adolph Streicher."

"There you are. Twins. How would Martigny know?"

"You're not a botanist, Pierre. What do you really do?"

"But I am a botanist. That is my vocation."

"What is your avocation?"

"I dig up graves."

"A ghoulish occupation."

"Someone has to do it," he said ironically.

"What is accomplished by opening graves?"

"It lets the stench out so the whole world can smell it."

"Is that necessary?"

"Have you ever visited any of the camps? Dachau, say, or Auschwitz?"

"No."

"They've been turned into something like your American Forest Lawn. Grass, trees, flowers. It's just that I don't think that Auschwitz should smell like a floral shop, even though I am a botanist. I want to restore the charnel-house stink. Do you understand?"

"I think so."

"The Streichers—you see, they aren't wholly a matter of revenge. They are just the instruments I use to open mass graves. You might call them the shovels and picks—no, the bulldozers. Trials, documents, testimony, newspapers and television, publicity—I try to encourage others to smell the stench that has been in my nostrils since I was fifteen years old."

"Who do you work for? *Shin Beth?*"

"The Israeli National Security Council? Certainly not."

"The Jewish Documentation Center?"

"No, although we communicate."

"Who, then?"

"It's odd, but I don't know how to answer your question. It would be arrogant of me to say I work for the dead and stupid to claim to work for the living. I don't think about it—I just work."

"Alone?"

"No. There is a small volunteer—what?—organization, network. Something like that. An informal group of Jews, Gypsies, Slavs—*Untermenschen.* You know, subhumans."

"And Adolph Streicher?"

"A mistake, I think. One of many. He is probably dead, as was originally reported. Still . . . how do you know? There was Eichmann, of course. And Dr. Mengele is living happily in Paraguay. We must investigate these rumors.

Most come to nothing, but now and then. . . . You see, we received several reports that Walter Streicher was really Adolph Streicher. It's possible. They were twins. Who would know? Family? Few family members survived the war, and if they knew, would they tell? Close friends? As far as we can tell, neither Walter nor Adolph Streicher acquired many friends. Even so, would they tell? I doubt it. And with identical twins, even friends might be deceived. So, this is mostly routine. We hear that perhaps the war criminal Adolph Streicher is living in Munich as his brother Walter Streicher. We ignore it for years, but then a woman who knew both of them, a neighbor who survived the camps and emigrated to Israel and then recently returned to Munich, tells us that Walter is not Walter, he is Adolph. We investigate. We must. But it is not necessarily so."

"Pierre, it wasn't an accident that you arrived here the day after Dieter Streicher."

"Of course it wasn't."

"You were following Dieter."

"Certainly."

"Did he know?"

"Yes. He cooperated, or pretended to cooperate. Dieter apparently was an anti-Nazi, even if his father was involved."

"I didn't know any of this."

"You weren't supposed to."

I picked up the wine bottle and started to pour some wine into a glass.

"Not that glass," Margolin said.

"Why not?"

"It contains a perfect set of fingerprints."

"But you said that identical twins were born with identical fingerprints."

"Well, you see, that was a lie."

"Do you lie often, Pierre?"

"Almost all the time," he said, laughing.

"Why follow Dieter?"

"It seemed simpler. It's sometimes difficult for us to work in Germany and Austria. But the boy, Dieter, might receive a letter. We have specimens of Adolph Streicher's handwriting. There might be fingerprints on the envelope or letter. And something incriminating might be said in such a letter. After all, Dieter was returning to the area of his father's crimes—mightn't his father comment on it?"

"And did you intercept any letters?"

"Three. One from his mother and two from a girl friend. But none from Walter-possibly-Adolph Streicher."

"Wasn't it a mistake to let Dieter know that you were hunting his father? And isn't it a mistake to let Walter know that you suspect he really might be Adolph?"

"We would learn something if he ran," he said. "And with a warm trail. . . ."

"All right, Pierre. You have been very candid. Now, though, I have the feeling that you intend to present me with the bill."

"More wine?"

"No."

"You don't have to cooperate."

"I know that."

"But perhaps you'll volunteer."

"I doubt that very much."

"Only three of us arrived at the first concentration camp," he said. "My sister had been trampled to death in the cattle truck that took us out of France. A younger brother died too during the trip, of I don't know what—thirst, asphyxiation, despair. My father, my mother and I arrived at the camp. The SS guard who lowered the truck tailgate said, 'Here you enter through the gate and exit through the chimney.' That was a favorite saying of the SS in all the camps. My father had arthritis and the camp doctors classified him unfit for work. He was exterminated almost immediately. That is, after he was examined and it was ascertained that he had several gold teeth worth recovering. My mother lasted three months and finally she was killed too. But first they shaved off her hair. Did you know that when Auschwitz was liberated they found about seven tons of human hair? No one could understand *why* the Germans had saved seven tons of hair. Later a document was found which explained that the hair was to be used to make slippers for the feet of German submariners."

"All right," I said.

"I was fifteen then, almost sixteen, and very strong, and so they put me to work."

"All right, Pierre."

"All right what?"

"What do you want me to do?"

"You're going into the mountains with Streicher tomorrow, I hear. Observe him for me. Don't ask any stupid questions. Don't play detective. Watch him, listen to what he says, catalogue his movements and gestures—and then tell me about it. When you return, tell me everything he's said and done during the whole time."

"Okay."

"Even the things that seem totally irrelevant, tell me."

I nodded.

"And it's possible, just possible, that at some time or another he'll take off his shirt in your presence. Adolph Streicher was in the SS and nearly every SS man had tattoos applied beneath his armpits. Blood type, serial numbers and so forth."

"You don't think he'd show anyone those tattoos?"

"The tattoos would be gone by now. But you might get a glimpse of scars that remained after tattoo removal."

"Anything else?"

"Be careful."

"Isn't that a little melodramatic, Pierre?"

"No."

"This Streicher doesn't seem very tough."

"Listen, my friend, toughness isn't a hardening of the muscles, it's a hardening of the soul. If this man is really Adolph Streicher, the first thing you'd learn about his toughness is the instant when he buried an ice axe in the back of your head."

"I'll watch him."

Margolin got up from the table. "I'm very tired and I've got a headache. Excuse me."

"You didn't eat your cucumber, Pierre," I said, smiling.

"That was a stage prop," he said. "Anyway, at one time the Germans classified me as an *Unnuetze's Esser.*"

"And what does that mean?"

"Useless eater." He smiled and left the room.

10

At noon the following day Streicher and I left the town of Argentière, at the east end of the valley, and began hiking up toward the Lognan refuge. It was a hot afternoon and the creeks had been turned into roaring, foamy torrents by glacier melt. It was hot even in the shade of the larch forest. We did not talk much. Our packs were heavy and the trail was steep and we had not yet found our rhythms. I followed behind and watched Streicher as he walked up the path's steep switchbacks. I could see that he was a strong and experienced hiker. He moved well. There was no hurry, no waste motion. He let his lower legs do most of the work. Each step was calculated to expend the least possible amount of energy. He chose a pace that appeared slow but which could be employed from dawn to dusk. Streicher plodded up the trail like a slow, stubborn automaton.

The forest thinned as we approached timberline. The trees were small and grotesquely twisted. More sunlight penetrated to the ground. We walked through splashes of sunlight, among the dwarfed, wind-crippled trees, and then we passed the last stunted tree and were walking through a field of rhododendrons. Below and to our left we could see the Argentière glacier. Ahead, misty in the afternoon haze, we saw some great, reddish-hued rock walls, the Verte, Les Droites, the snow-streaked Aiguille du Chardonnet.

There were some climbers lounging around the Lognan refuge. They watched us as we slogged by. We went on past the building and along a trail that was no more than a narrow terrace on the steep hillside. Ahead we could see a very broken section of the glacier. It was a jumbled maze, a crosshatching of deep crevasses and enormous séracs—ice blocks as big as a two-story building. The ice was dirty and littered with rocks carried down from higher levels, but here and there I saw sun-bright flashes of emerald and sapphire and amethyst. More great peaks were visible now, but even those that remained out of sight could be sensed, in the same way that a compass detects hidden metal. A tremendous weight seemed to burden the earth here.

"What do you see, Streicher?" I asked as we paused on the path.

He was silent so long I believed he did not intend to answer. Then: "Geology," he said. "I see time, billions of years. Mortality."

The path angled downward, and eventually we were on the glacier's lateral moraine.

At this altitude the glacier was bare of new snow. It was

a broken, split and shattered field of melting ice. Pools of water lay in all the hollows. There was a cool, damp smell. We stopped to put on sunglasses and smear our faces with glacier cream. Then we sat on a sun-heated boulder and I explained briefly to Streicher the proper uses of the rope in glacier travel, ice axe belays, how to stop a fall, and the complicated techniques of extracting a man from a crevasse if a fall did occur. I did not go into the subject very thoroughly; I just instructed him on a few of the basics and trusted that a knowledge of the rest would not be necessary. There was really little danger here: the crevasses were all visible and could easily be avoided. It might be different up high, where recent snowstorms had concealed some of them.

I uncoiled a two-hundred-foot length of nine-millimeter rope, doubled it to one hundred feet, and we tied on. Then I took in some coils and looped them over my chest so that there were only about forty feet between us. We didn't need the rope now, but I thought it would be good practice for Streicher. Tomorrow we would have to traverse more difficult terrain.

"Don't carry any loose coils in your hand," I said.

"I won't. I'll just run a single small coil around the shaft of my axe, as you told me."

"Keep the rope taut between us."

He nodded.

"Watch me. If you see me fall, jab your axe into the ice and hold on."

"All right."

We climbed over the moraine's rubble and stepped out on the ice. It was slushy on the surface and I sank nearly to midcalf. We started off. It was awkward, strenuous travel, and soon I was sweating. We jumped the smaller crevasses and detoured around the larger ones. The sun was brightly reflected off the ice, and even though I was wearing dark sunglasses I had to squint against the glare. My wool shirt became soaked through with sweat. Sweat diluted the glacier cream on my face, and it ran off in sticky rivulets. It was hot, tedious, miserable going. Twice I led us into cul-de-sacs and we had to retrace our steps. After a while the glacier steepened and became even more broken. There were huge séracs scattered about and I gave them safe margin. Sun melted the ice blocks and changed their precarious balance. It was very unhealthy to be near one when it collapsed.

The interiors of the crevasses were a cool luminous blue, and the color darkened as they went down. In some I could hear the echoing rush of melt water: blue canyon rivers winding their way downward through the frozen catacombs of ice. A hundred yards away a giant sérac toppled with a sound like the crack of thunder. The noise echoed and reechoed through the amphitheater, and the air was filled with powdery clouds of ice crystals that glowed blue and green in the sunlight.

After two hours we stopped for a rest. We sat on our rucksacks and drank water and smoked cigarettes. We were well into the long, narrow horseshoe-shaped basin that surrounded the glacier. Stone walls rose thousands of feet into the sky all around us. To our right was the Aiguille Verte and Les Droites, and ahead, Les Courtes. They were connected in a long granite chain streaked with ice couloirs and peaked by jagged pinnacles. To our left was the Aiguille du Chardonnet and its long, somewhat lower chain. Ahead was Mont Dolent, a border of three countries:

France, Italy and Switzerland. There was really only one comparatively easy way out of here, and that was by the route we had come.

"Oppressive," Streicher said.

"The heat?"

"The terrain. It crushes the spirit."

"Often it elevates the spirit," I said.

He sat on his rucksack and began peeling an orange. He looked like a comic-book illustrator's concept of a Martian: face streaked with white glacier cream, small round sun goggles protruding like insect eyes, nose a white lump with two small dark holes at the base, a wide, tense frog mouth.

"This Pierre Margolin," Streicher said, "is he some sort of policeman?"

"I don't know."

"There was no need for him to treat me like a criminal yesterday."

"Finish your orange. We still have a long way to go."

We had gained considerable altitude, and there was fresh snow from Saturday's storm on the surface of the glacier. The snow was wet and heavy and sometimes I sank in to my thighs. We were not so much walking now as we were plowing through the thick slush. The sun seemed bloated to twice its normal size, and it glazed the air with blurry heat mirages.

We reached the old refuge an hour before night. It was located on a broad, sloping platform of slab granite. A huge mound of boulders, remains of an ancient rockfall, protected it from avalanches. It was a small, crude hut built of reddish stones. Few climbers used it anymore. Most of the alpine huts were now more like small hotels, with two or three stories, large kitchens and a complete staff, comfortable dormitories and sun decks. This was really a hut, really a refuge.

We went inside. The floor was littered with debris. The room smelled musty and sour and there were rat turds in the corners. All of the furniture had long since been broken up and used for firewood.

We spent half an hour cleaning the place, and then I set up my butane stove and placed a saucepan of water on the burner. When the water began to boil I poured in a package of dehydrated chicken noodle soup mix, and then got my knife and sliced some cheese and bread. I took my food outdoors while Streicher remained behind in the hut.

I sat down on a rock and began eating. Most of the steep-walled cirque was in cool shadow now, although the higher peaks still blazed with sunshine. The sky looked as if it were being supported by the jagged pillars of ice and rock. I finished eating and lit a cigarette. Somewhere, far off, a sérac collapsed, and the dull explosion reverberated for five or ten seconds, echoed longer in my mind; and then silence rushed back like air into a vacuum.

Streicher came out and sat nearby.

"Tired?" I asked.

"Yes, tired and wet. Is there any way we can dry our boots and clothes?"

"No. You won't find any firewood out here."

He was silent for a time. "Tell me," he asked, "does this Margolin intend to cause me trouble? He was so hostile in a smiling way."

"I don't see how he can cause you any trouble if you really are Walter Streicher."

"I am."

"Well, then. . . ."

RON FAUST

Again he was silent. The last sunlight was extinguished on the higher peaks. It was growing dark and cold in the amphitheater.

"Ah," Streicher said suddenly, "everything they say about Adolph is true. I refused to believe it for a long time. I investigated, hoping to clear my brother's name—but it is all true. I know it's true, but I can't understand it."

I flipped my cigarette away.

"How can it be? We were identical twins. If he was evil, then I must be evil too. But I never deliberately harmed anyone. Do you understand it?"

I shook my head.

"We were identical twins; we were the same person in two bodies. The same spermatozoon fertilized the same egg. Our genes, our chromosomes. . . . *We were exactly the same.* He was Adolph and I was Walter. He was Walter and I was Adolph. We knew we were the same person. We were Adolph-Walter and Walter-Adolph. He was I and I was he. God, do you understand? We were exactly the same, and for twenty-two years we shared the exact same environment. We were always together, always. People couldn't tell us apart. Even those who could, our parents, treated us as one person. We shared everything, even punishment. Have you ever considered what it is like to have an identical twin, Mr. Holmes?"

"Not much. It must be a narcissistic experience."

"How could Adolph have become a criminal, a monster?"

"When did you separate?"

"Ideologically?"

"Ideologically, physically—whatever."

"Adolph joined the Nazi Party early in 1938."

"And you refused to join?"

"No, I *wanted* to join. I told you we were the same person. I shared Adolph's zeal for the Party. It was very exciting then. It was dynamic, powerful; it seemed a tidal wave of change that would unite and revitalize Germany. No, I believed passionately in the *Nationalsozialistische Deutsche Arbeiterpartei* then, like Adolph. We could not see what it would lead to. The lucid thinkers, the old German liberals like our father—they saw the adult tree in the seedling. But Adolph and I were only twenty-two years old. All we saw was the dynamism, the passion, the exultation of belonging to a Revolution that would awaken the world."

"Some of the passion seems to have remained," I said.

He smiled, showing his gray, crooked teeth. "No, I am just telling you how it was in 1938."

"German National Socialism was hardly a seedling in 1938. Why didn't you join the Party if it attracted you so much?"

"My father. Our father. As I said, he was an old German liberal. He certainly wouldn't be considered a liberal in any democratic nation of today. They would call him a reactionary, or maybe even a Fascist. I doubt if he could have been called a liberal in the England or America of 1938. He was a *German* liberal. But he despised the Nazis and the Communists equally. And he tried to dissuade us from joining the Party."

"And he half succeeded?"

"Yes. We had difficulty reconciling our own wishes with the demands of our father. We delayed, Adolph and I. We hoped that eventually our father would give us his permission, or even—miracle!—convert to National Socialism himself. You understand how it was then in patriarchal

Germany. One did not so carelessly revolt from authority as now. So we delayed and delayed. Adolph was in favor of joining the Party secretly. I wanted to wait for the right moment."

"And?"

"One day Adolph became angry and went off by himself and enlisted in the Nazi Party. That was really the first time that either of us had ever made any major decision alone."

"And you became angry?"

"Yes; furious, resentful, sullen. For twenty-two years we had been one person, and now he had acted like an individual."

"Individual action sounds healthy to me."

"You have never been a twin."

"That's right, and I'm beginning to feel grateful for it."

"I wanted to punish Adolph. I intended to join the Party, but first I wanted to cause him anguish."

"And did you?"

"Oh, yes. It is as easy to make a twin suffer as it is to make oneself suffer. You must know how easy that is. I wanted to make him sorry for his petty act of defiance. I became very cold and disapproving. I pretended to despise him. First I would punish Adolph and then I would absolve him."

"It worked?"

He shrugged. "In the usual way. The more you try to dominate a person, the more he rebels. I made him suffer, and his suffering drove him to greater defiance, and the defiance forced him into even greater acts of rebellion. And the more he rebelled, the more pressure I exerted on him. It continued to spiral. I made him suffer so much for joining

103

the Nazi Party without me that he went on and joined the *Schutzstaffel* without me. I made him suffer so much for joining the SS without me that on November ninth, 1938, *Kristallnacht,* he went out with some other thugs to burn synagogues and loot Jewish shops. That was insane. He had nothing against Jews. I punished him for that, too, of course. He became worse. I see it more clearly now—I understand that you hold people by letting them go."

"Or vice versa, according to your thesis. Go on."

"Adolph finally went off to Berlin. A few weeks later I enlisted in the Luftwaffe. I wanted to be a pilot. But the doctors found that I had poor night vision and so I was assigned to aircraft mechanics' school."

He sat quietly for a while, looking out at the gathering darkness. "I became a mechanic. Adolph became a murderer."

"I'm sure there's a moral," I said.

"No, no moral. That's just it. But sometimes I think I was saved because my name was Walter, not Adolph. I was born twelve minutes before Adolph, and so I was given my father's name. It's possible, isn't it, that I was slower to defy my father because I carried his name—just slightly more hesitant to join the Nazi Party because I carried the weight of a name and its tradition? And Adolph —he had a different name, a different inspiration. Do you think, is it really possible, that a name could determine a life?"

"I don't know, Streicher. Really, I'd like to help you. All I know is that one of you became a criminal and the other did not. I don't know that anything else matters much now."

"If *he* had been born first then he might have become a decent man because his name was Walter. And I. . . ."

"There's really no profit in all this Jesuitical dialectic," I said, smiling.

"We were the same person, but the *names*."

"Let's go to sleep now."

"Maybe if my name had been Erich and his name had been Peter we both would have joined the Luftwaffe. And we both certainly were deficient in night vision, and so both of us would have become mechanics."

I laughed. "Streicher, you're half crazy. You'd be wholly crazy, except that your twin brother is dead or living in South America. Let's go to sleep now. We have to get an early start tomorrow."

"It haunts me."

"What haunts you is the knowledge that you could just as easily have become a criminal."

"Of course. Since we were really the same person."

"And so Adolph became a loyal Nazi."

"A fanatic. Nazi dogma was higher than God's law to him. His passion increased, while mine diminished. And you know, there is some irony in the fact of Adolph's being a doctrinaire Nazi and being a twin too. Have you ever heard of Dr. Mengele?"

"Yes, recently."

"He was a doctor at Auschwitz. Among his uncounted crimes were the torture and murder of thousands of twins from all over Europe, many of them children. For example, he would have one twin tortured while across the compound he would observe the reactions of the other twin. I suppose he hoped that one twin would scream in agony while the other was flayed alive. Mengele has not yet published the results. And he also tried in various ways to turn brown eyes blue—chemical Aryans. He has not yet published these results either. And often he simply became bored and injected phenolic acid into his victims. Oh, yes, Dr. Mengele did pioneer work in studying twins. The Nazis were primitives, and like most primitives they were suspicious of twins. Double birth seems a violation of nature to the primitive mind—like albinos, or defectives, or even redheads. Many aboriginal tribes simply killed twins at birth. Mengele had a more practical approach. And no aborigine ever devised a policy of *Vernichtung lebensunwerten Lebens*—the annihilation of those who aren't worthy of life."

"Where is Mengele now?"

"Dr. Mengele is living in Paraguay."

"Maybe your brother Adolph is a neighbor. It could be that they get together every now and then and reminisce about the good old days. Finish the evening by torturing one of the kids from the *barrio*."

"I am very tired," Streicher said, slowly rising to his feet.

We went into the hut and began preparing for sleep. Streicher had a down sleeping bag, and he made his bed at the far end of the room. I had my down jacket and an elephant's foot, an emergency bivouac sack that came to the hips. I removed my wet boots, stockings and gaiters. They would be frozen stiff in an hour or so. I put on my jacket, pulled up the elephant's foot and lay on a thin foam pad. A pale gray underwater light filtered in through the windows. The walls of the hut were black, and after a few minutes I could not distinguish the windows from the walls. The night grew cold.

Streicher's voice echoed in the darkness. "I have set my wristwatch alarm for 2:00 A.M."

"That's about right," I said.

"Good night."

"Good night, Streicher."

"Call me Walter, please."

"Good night, Walter." I 80 percent believed now that he really was Walter.

11

Streicher's wristwatch alarm was a faint tinny clatter in the silence and darkness of the room. I opened my eyes. Moonlight defined the west windows and threw long, barred rectangles over the floor. I could hear Streicher moving around in the shadows at the far end of the hut. It was very cold. All I recalled of the past six hours was being cold. I switched on my flashlight and by its beam got my candle lantern and a new candle from my rucksack. I slid open the lantern, inserted the candle, lit it and lowered the wind shield. The candle flame was hardly brighter than the moonlight coming in through the windows, but I could save on flashlight batteries this way.

My boots, stockings and gaiters were frozen solid as I'd expected, and it was a miserable job getting dressed. Then I struck another match and got my butane stove

burning. The flame was a greenish blue and hissed loudly.
I placed a saucepan of water on the stove. "Coffee?" I
asked.

"Yes," Streicher replied.

"Two o'clock?"

"Two-ten, now." He came out of the shadows carrying
a candle. He looked thirty years younger in the soft candlelight, and for an instant I saw him as he must have been
once: a bony, angular face thinned to gauntness, sharp
features, alert eyes and a wide mouth that curved down
at the corners either in dejection or bitterness. He looked
like a young man for whom life would prove too harsh,
too brutal. But then he came closer, and his face fleshed
out and I could see the gray hair and the deeply etched
lines. He had survived and fattened.

We each had a cup of instant coffee and a piece of
bread, and then we picked up our rucksacks and went
outdoors. It was a fine cold night. We exhaled clouds of
vapor and looked around. Moonlight illuminated the glacier
and cast the surrounding peaks into sharp silhouettes.
There were a million stars. The night was so clear that
the stars possessed color: a dull red, a pale green, a delicate
blue. It was silent except for the groaning and creaking
noises deep in the glacier's ice-blue bowels.

We made our way through the talus to the glacier and
paused there to rope up. I was fully awake now and beginning to enjoy the night. The air was cold in my lungs
and nostrils.

Everything seemed new—the mountains and glaciers,
snow and ice, starlight, moon, shadows, cold, being alive.
It was all fresh. I felt new too, unused.

I led and Streicher followed forty feet behind me. The

crevasses were shady chasms against the moon-bright glacier surface. Our crampon points bit into the frozen snow. I heard the dry squeak of the snow being compressed; and my own breathing, and a grating noise from deep within the glacier. The moisture in my nostrils froze. It was very quiet, very cold. It was a strange sensation as always, like being the first to walk on an alien planet.

We came to a long crevasse and traversed leftward until I found a snow bridge. It was probably frozen solid, but to be safe I tested it with the spike of my axe. The spike penetrated for several inches and then struck hard ice. I continued probing. It seemed firm enough.

"It seems all right," I said to Streicher. "Belay me across."

Streicher jabbed the spike and shaft of his axe into the ice as deeply as it would go. He payed the rope out around the shaft, ready to stop me if the snow bridge should collapse, and then I was safely over and I belayed him across.

We moved quickly and within an hour had reached the small subsidiary glacier that led up to the base of the mountain wall. There was a chaotic area of séracs and crevasses and boulders where the two glaciers converged. I found a route through the maze, and then the glacier became smoother as it slanted upward at a thirty-degree angle. We had relatively easy going for about five hundred yards, and then the grade abruptly steepened. The angle increased to about fifty-five degrees. A glacier is always more broken where the angle changes. The slowly moving ice splits into seams that often run every which way; walls of ice form; enormous séracs are broken off and stand isolated on the slope. It is never wholly safe to pass

111

through such an area but the danger is minimized if the weather is cold, if the sun has not yet begun to melt and loosen the ice.

We paused below the icefall. It looked like an asymmetrical crystal city in the moonlight. Etienne, Dieter Streicher and I had passed this way less than a week ago, but it all looked unfamiliar to me now. Our tracks had been covered by the snowstorm. The moonplay of light and shadow ruined perspective and turned everything into a dimensionless abstract of whites and grays and blacks. I would have to find a route through the icefall in the same way that a rat finds its way through a maze—by trial and error.

"Streicher," I said, "this slope is pretty steep. Would you feel more secure if I chopped steps in the ice?"

"No, the crampon spikes bite in quite firmly. Anyway, I've skied slopes almost this steep."

"You're a super skier, then. Okay, we'll move simultaneously with a taut rope. But some of the crevasses may be covered over. If I happen to vanish before your eyes, don't just stand there observing the phenomenon or you'll join me a hundred feet down."

"I'll be alert."

"Don't permit the rope to become slack."

"I understand all of that," he said impatiently.

"Let's go then," I said. I cramponed up the slope and entered into the cold crystal city.

We wandered around in the bewildering ice catacombs for almost two hours. The moon declined behind the silhouetted mountains and we had to use our flashlights. We traversed back and forth across the slope, advancing a few yards here, retreating, advancing again up another

112

shadowy ice canyon, not quite lost and yet never quite
certain of where we were. The icefall was not more than
one hundred and fifty yards high, and the glacier at this
point about twice that distance in width, but it took us
two hours and perhaps two miles of zigzag walking to
reach the sloping plateau at the top. I tried to remember all
the details of the final, successful route, so that our descent
would be swifter and easier.

It was growing light when we reached the great crevasse
at the top of the steep section. The crevasse was thirty
feet wide in this area and extended nearly the entire width
of the glacier. The guide Alain Garnier believed that
Dieter's body would be found at the bottom of this crevasse.

I was inclined to agree with him. Except for the bergschrund, the crevasse at the base of the rock wall, there
were no very large crevasses above us. A body falling from
high on the face would probably land below the bergschrund and then bounce and slide down the two or three
hundred yards of slope until swallowed by this chasm.
That was not certain though; the body might have fallen
into a small crevasse higher up, or it could have been
catapulted over this crevasse and into the icefall below.

We sat down on our rucksacks below the crevasse and
nibbled at some dried fruit and cashews. Streicher got out
his stove and began melting snow for coffee.

"I didn't know it would be like this," he said.

"What do you mean?"

"So vast, so difficult. How will it be possible to find
Dieter's body in this wild place?"

"We'll do what we can," I said.

"Where do we begin?"

113

"The body might be in this crevasse. I'll go down and look around."

"It seems hopeless."

"Dieter's body wouldn't be the first that was never recovered."

False dawn rapidly changed into daylight. The sky took on a deep blue as we watched, and gave color and dimension to the terrain. The crystal city below us lost its magic. The terrific rock walls, those above us and those across the vast amphitheater, became clearly visible.

I looked up at the wall which Etienne, Dieter and I had climbed several days ago and which only I had survived. It was scarred by ice-choked ravines and pressure ridges and weather-smoothed facets. The summit rose several hundred feet above the adjacent ridges. The entire 2,500 feet could have been called a spire or pinnacle, except that technically it was a part of a chain of mountains; it did not stand alone.

I traced the route with my eyes. There was the difficult icy chimney that Cottier had led. There was the forty-foot-long layback and above it a short but exceptionally hard friction pitch; there was also the pendulum traverse. And there, more than halfway up the wall, was the big ledge where we had debated whether or not to continue.

"Where did Dieter fall from?" Streicher asked.

I pointed. "Close to the summit, almost directly above us."

"My God! What would remain of him then?"

"More than you might expect."

We drank our coffee and smoked cigarettes and then I stood up. "I'll go down now," I said.

"Listen, it must be dangerous—is it worth risking your life to recover the remains of a dead man?"

"It's not all that dangerous."

"We have only two hundred feet of rope. What if that's not enough to reach bottom?"

"There's a platform about sixty feet down. This crevasse collects snow from the upper slopes when they avalanche."

"What if the platform isn't strong enough to support your weight?"

"Then I'll come back up the rope, and Dieter's body will stay wherever it happens to be."

"But *how* will you ascend the rope? Are you strong enough to climb sixty feet of rope hand over hand?"

"Jesus, Streicher, you're starting to make me nervous. Assume, will you, that I know what I'm doing? I can get out of the goddamned crevasse."

"I'm sorry," he said.

I fixed some anchors for the rope. I drove both of our axes deeply into the ice about four feet apart and then placed a sixteen-inch ice screw nearby. I arranged a system of rope loops, one from each axe and another from the ice screw, so that if one or even two anchors failed, the third would hold; and then I tied one end of the climbing rope to the three loops. I tested the system, and everything seemed solid enough.

"How long will you be down there?" Streicher asked.

"I don't know. I'll explore as much of the crevasse as I can. If I don't find the body I'll come up, and maybe we'll try again farther to the south."

"Is there anything I can do?"

"Sure. Keep an eye on the anchors. Get a suntan. Don't wander around and fall into a crevasse."

I got into rappel position and backed toward the opening. The upper lip of the crevasse was overhanging and I dangled free in the air for a moment below it, but then I slid down the rope a few feet, and my crampons came in contact with the ice wall. As soon as I passed down between the ice walls I felt a new cold, a damp, ice house cold. I could taste the cold. I could see my exhalations.

Melting and refreezing had made the outer surface of ice as smooth and brittle as eggshell. It shattered beneath my crampons, and I could hear the shards tinkling away below me with a sound like wind chimes. I slowly descended. Above me now the overhanging lips of the crevasse were a translucent blue green. Light was refracted inside the ice, twisted and broken into facets and glowing emerald blurs and phosphorescent starbursts—pure blue and green crystalline geometry. Farther down the color faded. The ice was a milky blue color with faint rainbow traces of violet and purple. Then almost all color was gone, and I was moving down into a dim cavern of gray marbled ice. It was twilight here. Above, on the glacier's surface, day was just beginning, but here it was the moment before night.

I touched down on the platform sixty feet beneath the surface. It felt solid underfoot. I shifted my weight gradually from the rope to the platform. It held, it was strong. I looked up and down the narrow cavern. The ice floor extended about forty feet to my left and perhaps eighty feet to my right. It was not smooth or level. There were ice blocks, frozen mounds, depressions, but it all looked solidly frozen, and so I decided to take a chance and abandon the rope.

I went to my left first, picking my way over and through the ice debris until I reached the end of the gallery. I lay down flat on the ice and looked over the edge. The crevasse dropped another fifty feet here. Very little light filtered down to that level, and the cavern below me was just a mass of bluish-black shadows.

I got out my flashlight. The conical beam pierced the darkness. The snow on the bottom had not been disturbed. Dieter's body could be lying beneath the snow, buried beneath a recent avalanche, but there was no way of determining that without descending with a shovel and digging up the tons of snow. I examined the crevasse as far as my flashlight could penetrate and saw nothing but ice and snow. The sculptured, fissured ice walls reflected the light and exhaled a damp cold.

I got to my feet and cramponed along the ice platform toward the far end. I was cold now. I was cold and hungry and tired and discouraged. It did not seem possible to find the body. The mountains were too big, the glaciers too rugged and seamed. Men had vanished forever in this kind of country.

I walked to the far rim and lay down. Ice reflected the flashlight beam with milky radiance. It was the same here as at the other end of the platform: snow and ice choking the lower levels of the crevasse, ice walls sculptured into smooth abstract forms by pressure and melt. I flashed the light through the dark, blue-black shadows. Nothing, nothing; it was hopeless.

I was about to get up when the light skimmed across a dark object. I lost it, and moved the light around in smaller circles until I found it again. It was darker than the ice, darker than the shadows—a climbing boot sticking up out of the snow at a forty-five-degree angle. I could see the cleated rubber sole and a few inches of the leather uppers. Lace hooks reflected the light. Against the odds I had found Dieter, but I was not in the mood to call it luck.

117

I was even a little disappointed. This was as appropriate a burial place as any climber was likely to inherit. It seemed pointless to return him to the lowlands now. But that was sentimental, romantic. It really didn't matter at all whether a man was buried beneath six feet of earth or one hundred and thirty feet of ice.

A steep ice ramp led into the long narrow cave below. I backed down the ramp, balancing carefully, kicking the front points of my crampons into the ice with each step; and then I reached the uneven floor of the room. I was far below the glacier's surface now. The crevasse went down even farther, but this whole section had been choked with avalanche snow. Very little light penetrated this far. I advanced fifteen yards down the cavern and shone my flashlight on the boot. It looked like Dieter's. I could see a part of the gaiter now, too. Dieter had been wearing red gaiters.

I tried to dig into the snow with my hands, but it had been consolidated into a mass nearly as hard as concrete. It had been foolish of me not to have taken one of the ice axes down here. I removed my rucksack and got out the candle lantern and my piton hammer. The hammer had a curved four-inch pick at one end. I then lit the candle and set the lantern down on a snow mound. It spread a circular glow which enclosed me and the boot.

I began digging. The snow-ice fractured into lumps. I dug for a while and then scooped out the lumps with my hands. It was hard, macabre work. I had seen the corpses of men who had fallen a long distance. Most of their bones had been broken, of course, and the skulls exploded upon impact. The muscle and flesh and viscera had been turned into a kind of jelly that was contained by the tough human skin. Soft, watery, unresilient jelly. You could never forget touching a body like that. But I knew that Dieter would be solidly frozen now, as hard as the ice surrounding him, and so at least that horror was averted.

It took me thirty minutes to clear the leg. I started digging to the left and within another twenty minutes had partially excavated what I believed to be his other leg. I had that leg cleared almost to the knee when it suddenly struck me that this leg was wearing a smaller, different style of boot than the other, and the gaiter was blue, not red.

I hurriedly retreated to the far end of the cavern and lit a cigarette. I felt the hair on my head and arms bristle. "Jesus!" I said, and the echoing ice walls whispered back at me. Forty-five feet away the circular candle glow shone on the two different legs.

12

I left the rucksack and my candle lantern and cramponed up the ramp to the platform. I needed an ice axe since it seemed as though this were turning into a mass disinterment. The sun was higher and there was more light now. The edges of the crevasse were green-glowing, the same color as the luminous dial of a watch, and the long slit of sky was a dazzling blue. I felt an instant of pleasure, of relief, at coming up out of the dark tomb below, but then I saw that the rope was being drawn upward.

"Streicher!" I shouted. "Streicher, leave the rope alone!"

The rope continued sliding up the wall, faster now.

"Streicher! Goddamn it, what are you up to?"

I scrambled down the rough platform and leaped for the end of the rope, but it was just beyond reach. I watched it crawl up the wall and vanish.

I stood silently for a time, and then I said, "Streicher, what are you doing? I'll get you for this, you son of a bitch. Be assured that I will."

A noise from above—snow being compacted underfoot. Then a shadow could be seen through the translucent rim of the crevasse. The shadow slowly divided and the detached part moved forward, appeared beyond the rim, blotting out some of the light, falling. I rushed off to one side just before Streicher hit the platform. He fell fifty feet with the loose-limbed, uncontrolled drop of a rag-stuffed dummy. He hit the ice, bounced a foot or so and then lay still. The right side of his head was bloody. There was a hole just forward of his ear, and dark blood and brains welled up out of the hole. Sticky, grayish pink membrane clotted in his hair. His open eyes did not reflect any light; already they were dull and gluey.

I turned and rushed down the platform and descended the ramp to the cavern below. I retrieved my piton hammer, blew out the candle and retreated until my back was against the cold ice wall. I waited there in the silence and darkness, looking up toward the blur of light at the top of the ramp. My heart was beating in an unnatural rhythm. I could smell my own sweaty fear. I remained there for at least half an hour, and then it occurred to me that whoever had killed Streicher might not necessarily want to kill me. He had pulled up the rope instead of using it to descend. No doubt he was gone now. I exhaled slowly and relaxed my grip on the piton hammer. And then, weak and nauseated from a body full of unused adrenalin, I realized that I might have been murdered as surely as Streicher. The rope was gone. It could well prove impossible to climb out of the crevasse.

I gathered up my rucksack and the candle lantern and climbed the ramp to the platform. The crevasse far above me glowed in pure aqua blues and greens. There was no sound from the surface. I went down the ice ramp to where Streicher lay. I didn't know where to start, and so I arbitrarily decided to start with him. I peeled off his down jacket. It might be useful later on. And then, since his jacket was off, I went ahead and removed his wool shirt and the wool fishnet underwear top. His body was loose and easy enough to manipulate, but I did not look at his eyes or the wound in front of his ear. I did look at the bare skin of his arms and underarms. There were no scars. This was Walter Streicher, then, according to Margolin. The poor bastard.

I removed his watch and strapped it around my left wrist. It might help the morale to know the time. It was 10:30 A.M. now. I then went through his pockets but there was nothing useful—a wallet containing money in francs and marks, identity papers, a photograph of Dieter when he'd been a child, a yellowed clipping from a Munich newspaper concerning the search for his twin brother Adolph, a canceled ticket to the Olympic boxing matches, a tube of lip balm, a key ring.

I grasped Streicher's ankles and dragged him down the platform. The body slid fairly easily over the ice. A thin, dotted trail of blood and brains was left behind. I paused for a rest at the edge of the ramp and then pushed him over into the echoing dimness. He slid rapidly down the chute, vanished, and I heard the body hit bottom. He joined his nephew and the stranger. This goddamned hole in the ice was turning into a refrigerated mass tomb. I only hoped that I did not join them in the fraternity of death. It

123

then occurred to me that Streicher might have been technically alive; I had not checked for pulse or respiration. I hesitated, turned and went back down the platform. It didn't matter. He was a dead man whether or not the body processes continued for a while longer.

I overturned my rucksack and emptied out my pockets. The butane stove: I could melt ice for water and tea. A little food: a can of sardines, a piece of cheese, dried bread, a chocolate bar, half a bag of cashews, three slices of dried apricot, a tiny plastic-enclosed cube of honey. Seven cigarettes and a book of matches. My flashlight. *Cagoule* and the half-length sleeping bag. The candle lantern with one half-burned candle and one spare. A couple of rock pitons, three aluminum karabiners. The piton hammer—God have mercy on me if that hammer broke, because no one or nothing else would.

The only thing to do now was to chop a stairway to the surface of the glacier. I was reluctant to begin, because the sooner I started the sooner I might learn that I was imprisoned here.

I picked up my piton hammer and swung the pick end into the wall with all the strength of my arm and shoulder. The ice fractured into a spider web of cracks with the first blow, and with subsequent blows I carved out a hollow that would hold my cramponed boot to the instep. I immediately began another step eight inches above and slightly to the left of the original step. I chopped a third step and a fourth and then paused to rest. I was sweating now despite the damp chill of the crevasse.

I smoked a cigarette and then cut handholds in the ice, one for each of the steps. I made them about three inches deep and wide, with a raised forward rim that I could curl

124

my fingers around. Then I could do nothing more from the ramp; I would have to ascend the steps in order to reach high enough to carve more steps. The difficulty was already increasing. It would increase in geometrical ratio as I moved up the ice wall. Geometry might kill me up near the overhanging lip of the crevasse.

I mounted three of the steps, grasped a handhold with my left hand and began chipping away at the ice. It was a strain, and I had to descend twice for rests before I finished the step. It was not as big or as secure as the others, but it would do. I then chipped out a handhold above the last step and descended again to the platform. The muscles in my shoulder were twitching and jumping. Bright sunlight spilled over onto the west wall of the crevasse. Melt water trickled down the ice and froze again when it reached shade. It became like a greenhouse: damp, sultry, hot, oppressive. I felt as though I were breathing an equal mixture of water and air.

By three o'clock in the afternoon I was one-third of the way to the surface, but I did not know if I had the strength to finish the job. I was hungry and very tired. My arm muscles jumped and knotted. There was an intermittent cramp in my left calf, and the long thigh muscles of both legs were hard and burning. I could trace the raised muscles with my fingers.

I stopped then for an hour and brewed some tea and ate the cheese and sardines on the last of my bread. I smoked another cigarette and then resumed work.

It was almost dark when I had finished hacking out a stairway halfway to the surface. The light filtering in through the opening was gray and feeble. All the greens and blues had been drained out of the ice. Everything was gray, cold, hard. The last light went swiftly. It was almost as if it had been sucked up out of the crevasse in one giant inhalation—dusk and then night, without an interval between. And it quickly became cold. My sweat evaporated and I was shivering miserably in the darkness. My mind split into factions and engaged in war. The same old war: hope versus despair.

All day long I had heard the soft grinding of the glacier, but now, freezing again, it creaked and groaned, and cracked with a shrill reverberating ping. Silence, and then it thundered. I had heard these sounds before, but then I had been on the surface. Down here, inside the glacier, the noises were amplified to a ghastly, deafening din. I flicked on my flashlight, and it seemed that the walls had closed. No, that was impossible. Crevasses do not open and close so rapidly. The glacier squeaked, grated, and then thundered again. Loosened ice rattled down the wall. Silence, a very long silence . . . waiting . . . and finally a prolonged shriek like a human screaming.

I lit the candle lantern. A thin blade of flame rose, wavered, then bloomed into a white glow that was reflected off the walls. I got a rock piton from my rucksack, clasped the end of the lantern's chain between my teeth and ascended the ice ladder. I hammered the piton into the ice and hung the lantern from it. Then I began chopping out another step. I had almost finished when a cramping thigh muscle forced me to descend.

I sat down on my rucksack and looked up toward the candle glow. Ice returned the light with a clear blue-green fire. The steps and handholds ran halfway up the wall. I would have to be very careful not to slip. A fifty-foot fall, a twenty-foot fall onto the cement-hard platform would certainly put me out of action. So now I would have to take a lot of time and cut a secure stairway to the top of the crevasse. The lip looked like a big curling ocean wave that had been frozen at the instant of breaking. I intended to cut a vertical channel up through the overhang. That was when the danger of falling would be greatest. And, of course, there was always the chance that the entire ice cornice would fracture and collapse on me.

I went back up the steps and resumed chopping at the ice. I worked at it most of the night, often pausing to rest, and when the first gray light of false dawn oozed down into the crevasse I had carved a stairway to the base of the overhang.

I descended, lit the butane stove and began melting ice chips for tea. I was badly dehydrated: no matter now violently I worked I did not perspire. I was nauseated, my muscles were cramping from salt deficiency, and I was totally exhausted. There was a timelag between my brain's commands and my body's response. My reflexes were gone: it would have taken me two seconds to pull my hand out of an open flame. But I was close to the top now. The hardest work was yet to come; still I believed that somehow I'd find the resources to finish the job.

I remember drinking a cup of tea and then putting more ice chips into the saucepan. I remember lighting a cigarette. That is all I can remember until I awakened in the hot, bright, blue crevasse. It was almost ten o'clock. The ice shone with a deep blue fire. The cigarette had burned a hole in my wool knickers. It had also burned my thigh. The stove's cartridge had run out of butane and a crust of ice had formed on the water. I had slept almost five hours, but I did not feel particularly refreshed.

127

I loosened my stiff muscles with isometrics and then ascended the stairway to begin chopping a channel through the overhang. It was much easier than I had expected. Warmth had softened the ice and it broke away in large chunks. I chopped until my arms trembled and my legs cramped, and then I carefully descended the steps to rest again. After about twenty such trips I descended for the last time. The channel, first a three-sided trench in the ice and then a three-foot vertical shaft large enough to enclose my body, broke through into the sunlight.

I gathered all of my things, stuffed them into the rucksack, slipped my arms through the straps, and climbed the steps, and then very carefully edged my way up the channel.

There was a moment of claustrophobia when my upper body was surrounded by ice, but then I reached out and placed my palms flat on the glacier surface and pulled myself up. The sunlight was blinding. I put on my dark glasses, stood up and looked around. There were many tracks in the snow. The two ice axes, the ice screw and Streicher's rucksack were gone. The murderer had probably thrown them into another crevasse. Splashes of dried blood darkened the snow crust.

It was dangerous to walk down through the icefall at this hour, but I had no intention of waiting here until tonight's frost. If a sérac fell on me, it fell. If a snow bridge was softened by the sun and I dropped through it into another crevasse, so be it.

I started walking. All I had to do was walk down the bright, hot, broken, crevassed, sun-glazed glaciers to the Arve valley. It was easy. I executed it in the pure, classical style, placing one foot ahead of the other and then lurching after it. I fell three or four times. My vision dimmed and blood pounded in my ears like the throbbing of far-off dynamos. But it was always possible to take one more step, and by a series of thousands of just-one-more-steps I made it to that sweet-smelling, mysterious place of green and growing things.

13

It was night when I reached the pension. Christiane was working in the kitchen when I entered; and she turned to look at me over her left shoulder. She was wearing blue jeans and a light sweater, and her black hair was tied in a ponytail and her dark brown eyes were flecked with gold. She dried her hands on a small towel and turned.

"How did it go?" she asked.

I dropped my rucksack on the floor, shrugged and sat down.

"You're terribly sunburned."

I touched my raw, hot face. "Do I look older?"

She moved closer. "No. The same, about forty-five."

"I'm thirty-five."

She laughed and sat down next to me. "Tell me about it. Did you find the young German's body?"

"No."

"I didn't think you would. It's so big, so difficult out there."

"Yes."

"Where is that Walter Streicher?"

I thought about where Walter Streicher was.

"Isn't he coming?"

I was too tired to think clearly. I was exhausted and confused and a little paranoid. Two Streichers had been killed within a few days and I had been associated with both of them. I had been the next to the last person to see them alive. I decided to be evasive, at least until morning, when I could sort out my options sensibly.

"He's staying elsewhere tonight."

"Why?"

"He realized that he wasn't welcome here."

"Good. Jules will come back now."

"Where is Jules?"

"I don't know."

"And Margolin?"

"I don't know where he is, either. Are you hungry?"

"Yes, but I'm too tired to eat now. Could I raid the kitchen in four or five hours?"

"Of course. Let me know and I'll prepare something. If I'm still awake."

"Thank you. Is there hot water?"

She nodded, smiling faintly.

"And wine?"

"Yes, there is wine, too."

"May I take a bottle upstairs with me?"

"Yes, certainly."

"You're very kind to a weary old man."

"It will appear on your bill."

"The kindness?"

"The wine and maybe the kindness too," she said, smiling.

"You have room service?"

"Some kinds of room service," she said mockingly. "This is a small pension and we can't provide everything for the satisfaction of our guests."

"What kinds of room service do you provide?"

"You will have to make specific inquiries."

"Will you come upstairs and scrub my back while I bathe?"

She laughed. "I think your back will stay dirty."

"Will you give me a massage?"

"You have massage on the brain. I think you are a little kicky in that respect."

" 'Kinky' is the word. Although probably I'm a little 'kicky' too. In that respect. Will you at least come with me to the room and turn down the covers of my bed?"

"You are not nearly tired enough, I see. I will give you the bottle of wine and my felicitations."

"I'll dream about you."

"I really don't care to appear in your erotic dreams." She rose from the table, went down to the cellar and returned a moment later with a bottle of red wine.

I compelled my aching muscles and bones and tendons to perform the hundred separate tasks necessary to get me to a standing position. They collaborated badly and I almost fell back again. I accepted the bottle of wine and then put my arms around her and kissed her. She did not

133

resist. She returned my kiss and remained pressed close to me. I released her and stepped back. Her eyes were cool and laughing.

"Go take your bath," she said.

"And then what?"

"And then you'll probably smell sweeter."

"And?"

"And nothing. Go away."

I went slowly up the stairs and into the bathroom. I undressed and ran the tub full of hot water. I uncorked the wine and lit a cigarette while the water was running. Then I stretched full length in the tub, submerged except for my head and hands. In my right hand I held the burning cigarette and in my left the bottle of wine. I alternated sips of wine and inhalations of smoke. Vice is so much more pleasurable when you have earned it through suffering and sacrifice. One vice was missing, though—Christiane.

When the cigarette burned down to the filter, I placed the wine bottle on the floor and fell asleep. My dreams returned me to the crevasse. I chiseled incessantly at the hard ice walls. The glacier groaned and creaked and thundered. Deeper in the crevasse the two Streichers and the other corpse rustled through the snow and clawed at the ice and whispered to each other—an incomprehensible language of the dead.

Cold possessed me. I woke in the bathtub full of cool water. I drained the tub and refilled it with steaming hot water and then again fell asleep.

I remember little after that except a misty vision of myself crawling between the sheets of the bed. I recall that the blue-tinted sheets resembled glacier ice and I expected to meet a cold hardness, but it was soft, so very soft, and I sank downward, falling, and went to sleep before striking bottom.

I was awakened by a gentle tapping at the door. It was after ten o'clock according to Streicher's watch. The tapping again, louder now.

"Who is it?" I asked.

"Christiane."

"Just a minute." I turned on the bedside lamp, slipped into my knickers and crossed the room. I opened the door and she entered carrying a plate that contained cheese, bread and fruit. "That's nice of you," I said. "Thanks."

"The police were here," she said. "They wanted to see you."

"The police? When?"

"About two hours ago. I told them you were out."

"Why did you tell them that?"

"Because you were very tired. You needed sleep." She walked over to the table, set the plate down and then turned. "Have you done something wrong?"

"Nothing that I know of."

"Close the door," she said. "Pierre is in his room across the hall now."

I shut the door. "When did he return?"

"This evening. About an hour after you."

"Is Jules back yet?"

"No."

"Would you like a drink?" I asked her.

"Yes, please."

"Cognac or Scotch?"

"Scotch, please, with water."

I made two drinks, gave her one and then sat down

on the edge of the bed. "How many policemen were there?"

"Two."

"What did they want?"

"To see you. When I told them you were out they told me to inform you to go to the Préfecture tomorrow morning. Early. And they took your passport."

"You gave them my passport?"

"I had to."

"What else did they tell you?"

"Nothing. You know the police."

I sipped my drink.

"Is it serious?" she asked.

"No, I'm sure it isn't."

She looked around the room. "The place is a mess. Don't you ever put anything away?"

"Rarely."

She laughed. "You look very odd, wearing knickers and nothing else. Your face and hands are burned very dark and the rest of your skin is the color of a fish's belly."

"You know how to set a mood," I said. "Would you like another drink?"

"Yes, why not? Yes. I feel like getting drunk."

"Why?"

"Because I'm bored with sobriety. I'm bored with everything. Are we going climbing together soon?"

"Yes." I took her glass and stood up.

"Wait. There is some ice downstairs. I'll get it. Do you have enough to drink here, or should I get some wine?"

"There's half a bottle of Scotch and a nearly full bottle of good cognac. If they don't work we'll send out for a bottle of ether."

136

"And a pizza."

"Do you have any grass?"

"No, I'm just a simple provincial girl. I have a radio, though—we'll listen to music."

"We don't want to disturb Pierre."

"Of course we want to disturb Pierre. What is the sense of a party if no one is disturbed?"

"Are you going to stay the night?"

"I planned to, yes." She got up and walked toward the door.

"I hope you won't be bored," I said.

She turned, smiling. "I suppose that is up to you."

"*D'accord,*" I said.

14

The radio was still on when I awakened, and a nasal voice was celebrating the *honneur* and *grandeur* and *gloire* that were France. The radio was tuned much too loud. It had been blaring for hours, and when I turned it off the silence seemed unnatural.

Christiane, naked, sleeping, lay stretched next to me. Her long body was warm and soft and smooth. A screen of hair obscured her features. One hand was innocently cupped over her mons veneris, protecting that area from further assault.

Light streamed in through the window. I sorted through the mess of bottles and glasses and stinking ashtrays until I found Streicher's wristwatch: 9:20. It seemed best to go to the Préfecture rather than having the Préfecture come to me.

I got out of bed and began dressing. I was still tired from digging my way out of the crevasse. It felt as if all of my muscles and tendons and ligaments had shrunk and now I had the skeleton of a man six feet two inches tall and the musculature of a man five feet eight. I was like a bow that had been drawn much too tight.

Jules Martigny had returned. He was working in a field a hundred feet from the chalet. He paused and watched me as I crossed the yard and mounted my motorcycle. I kicked it over, and while the engine was warming I watched Martigny watching me. He leaned on the handle of his scythe and stared at me. He watched me turn the bike down the wagon ruts, and just before I curved into the trees I glanced in the rear view mirror and he was still watching me.

While riding toward Chamonix I tried to figure out how to deal with the police. I did not know why they wanted to see me. It was obviously more serious than I'd indicated to Christiane. They would not have confiscated my passport if it was related to a simple inquiry regarding the accident that had killed Cottier and Dieter Streicher. I did not see how it could be related to the murder of Walter Streicher. Who knew about that except me and the killer? And the killer was hardly likely to notify the police. No doubt the sensible thing would be to report the murder of Walter and also tell of my suspicions about Dieter's death. If I were in America or England or Switzerland or any of a half dozen other countries, that is exactly what I would have done. But this was France. Here you were guilty until proven innocent. They had preventative detention. They locked you up first, and then began gathering evidence. The police and judiciary

140

worked together like the thumb and forefinger of the same hand. The trials were sometimes as well rehearsed as a Comédie-Française play.

I decided to lie until it was clear what the police wanted with me. If I immediately told the truth it would be impossible to lie later, whereas if I lied first I could always tell the truth afterward. This seemed to make a complicated sort of sense at the time.

I parked my bike close to the Préfecture and went inside. After a thirty-minute wait I was led down the corridor to Guillot's office. He was seated behind his desk as before, but today he did not rise to greet me, nor did he offer me his hand, nor did he suggest that I have a glass of plum brandy. He told me to sit down and put out my stinking cigarette.

He tugged at his heavy lower lip and looked at me. His expression was genial enough, but that was only because of the natural set of his features, the mismatched lips, potato nose, bright eyes and the acute slant of his eyebrows. He would probably look at you in the same mistily affectionate way while he cut out your heart and ate it.

"Are you familiar with Napoleonic law?" he asked.

"Not as familiar as I think I should be," I said.

"Yes," he said, smiling. "Well, as long as you understand that you are not shielded by the United States Constitution and the Bill of Rights."

"I understand that."

"As an individual, there are many things I admire about English and American law."

"Me too."

"But as a policeman . . ."

"I understand."

141

"Actually, of course, the American Revolution learned a great deal from our Revolution."

"I don't think so."

"You don't think so?"

"The American Revolution preceded the French Revolution."

"You are wrong," he said. He placed his elbows on the desk and linked his pink sausage fingers together. "Do you have a new watch?"

I glanced at Streicher's wristwatch. "Yes."

"What happened to the one you were wearing Sunday?"

"You're very observant. It isn't working."

"May I see that one?" His gaze was soft and candid.

I removed the watch and handed it to him across the desk.

"It doesn't look new," he said. "A good watch—made in Germany."

"Switzerland."

"Yes, that's right, Switzerland." He looked at the back of the watch. "There is an inscription. 'To W.S. from F.S.' Why is that engraved on the back of your watch?"

"There is no inscription," I said.

He smiled and handed me the watch. I strapped it around my wrist, fighting the urge to look and see if there really was an inscription.

"Streicher was here to see me Monday. He was wearing a watch very much like that one."

"The company makes thousands of them," I said.

"No doubt."

My passport was on his desk. Next to it was an eight-by-eleven-inch manila folder with my name printed on the cover. Guillot seemed astonished by the coincidence of finding them on his desk. He looked at the passport and then at the folder and then at me, and he smiled as if he simply could not believe in his good luck at finding so much order in his disorderly world.

"You went into the mountains with a German national Tuesday."

"That's right."

"A relative of the Streicher boy."

"Yes."

"His father, in fact—Adolph Streicher."

"No."

"No?" A Gallic pursing of his mismatched lips.

"Walter Streicher, Dieter's uncle."

"Now, now," he said. "We've received a dozen telephone calls and visits during the past two days informing us that the Nazi criminal Adolph Streicher was in this area. Reliable informants, men and women who had good reason to remember the man, have told us that they saw and recognized him. Jules Martigny told us that Adolph Streicher was staying at his pension. Alain Garnier—you remember Alain—was at the Lognan refuge Tuesday afternoon and he saw you and this Streicher pass by. And others, eight or ten others, have possibly identified the man. Anatole Roue, a railroad employee who was tortured by Streicher personally many years ago, came to see us. Apparently he returned to this valley because of the death of his son."

"The man was Walter Streicher, Adolph's twin brother."

"Adolph Streicher had a twin?"

"Yes."

"Where ever did you hear such a thing?"

"Isn't it true?"

"How do I know if it's true? It's something you've just told me."

"The man was Walter Streicher."

"How do you know?"

"Because he told me and—"

"*He* told you!"

"And because Pierre Margolin knew that Adolph Streicher had a twin brother, and he believed that this man was Walter."

"Ah, yes, Margolin. The free-lance avenger, the conscience of Europe. So Margolin is interested in this man."

"Yes."

"But why, since he believes him to be the twin?"

"Well, he had a slight doubt."

"A slight doubt only."

"The man was Walter Streicher, not Adolph."

"Tell me, why is it that I use the present tense and you the past tense as we discuss this man?"

I shrugged. "Habit."

"That's right, you are sometimes a journalist. Have you found work?"

"Yes."

"How unfortunate. In journalism?"

"Yes."

"Oh, well, that isn't too serious. All one needs to practice that craft is a dark bar with a telephone."

Guillot opened my dossier (which I believed, and hoped, was empty), peeked inside and then quickly closed it, as if he had glimpsed something distasteful inside; a spider, say, or a crushed cockroach.

"Now," he said, "Pierre Margolin is a friend of yours."

"An acquaintance."

"Do you work for him?"

"Of course not."

"Do you know what his work is?"

"Pierre is a botanist. And he traces German war criminals."

"Sometimes he traces what he considers to be French war criminals as well. He traces them right up to the borders of the Beyond."

"He told me he stays within the law."

"Pierre is an expert liar. As you are, my friend."

"Are you saying Margolin is a violent man?"

Guillot linked his fingers behind his head, leaned back in the swivel chair and consulted the ceiling. "During the Algerian business some years ago, when plastic bombs were detonating all over Paris, a peculiar thing was noted—among all the terror bombings and murders there seemed to be a number which were very selective. Say that a distinguished judge's automobile was blown up and the judge killed. It might be known by the police that this particular judge had, during the Occupation, worked anonymously for the Nazis. Most of our judges did remain anonymous then, for protection.

"And then perhaps a police official was killed by a sniper while picnicking in the country. It turns out that the policeman had worked for the Gestapo during the Occupation, helping to round up Jews. Then, possibly, a medium-level politician or trade union leader was *plastiqued* out of this world while enjoying a sauna bath. The records might reveal another wartime collaborator."

"Interesting," I said.

"In the general chaos, the aimless violence, some personal grievances could be settled."

"Were they so personal?"

"Our government claims they were."

"And you think Margolin was responsible for these murders?"

"The Sûreté thought so."

"Why wasn't he arrested then?"

"He could not be found."

"And now?"

"It's long past, it's over, and there is little evidence. And it does seem that Pierre has behaved himself since then. But if he is starting over again, we'll crush him."

"Well," I said, "I don't know. Why were these judges and police officials and politicians and unionists permitted to go unpunished for their activities during the Occupation?"

He shrugged. "There were trials after the war. Many were punished, a great many—one of our periodic bloodbaths. Some escaped because of their anonymity, others because they were so insignificant, and some because no amount of chaos and misery, no cataclysm, can break up the power cliques. It sometimes appears that the most powerful were the most eager collaborationists."

"Do you mind if I smoke?" I asked.

"Yes," he said. He leaned over my passport again. "And also, nearly everyone in France shared the guilt. We are all tainted. You cannot understand that unless you've gone through it."

"I see."

"Now, you went into the mountains Tuesday with Adolph Streicher."

"Walter Streicher."

"And you returned last evening. Alone."

"Yes."

"I have been very open with you, very candid." He showed me his big meaty palms. "No American rubber hoses, no bright lights, just this mutual confidence. Correct? Now, where is Adolph Streicher? He is wanted by our government for crimes committed against the French people. Would you want to interfere with justice?"

"Walter Streicher."

"Where is he?"

"Give me my passport."

"No. I shall keep it for a while."

"What are you setting me up for, Guillot?"

"I am losing my patience," he said.

"Walter Streicher crossed over into Switzerland."

He gazed at me fondly, as a father might regard a favorite son who has perpetrated some charming piece of mischief. "Yes," he said. "Yes."

"We met two Swiss and he went with them."

"Oh, God," he said, "this is delightful."

"You asked me."

"Why did he go off with these two Swiss?"

"He believed he was in danger in this valley because people had mistaken him for his brother."

"And so he went to Switzerland," Guillot said dreamily.

"Yes."

"Where did you separate?"

"On the Argentière glacier."

"And Streicher went off with two Swiss. Like that."

"Yes."

"How did they go to Switzerland?"

"I assume they went up to the end of the basin and climbed Mont Dolent or one of the ridges and then descended into Switzerland. Or Italy, perhaps."

147

"Or Italy, perhaps. You assume, yes. Did you know these Swiss?"

"No."

"Would you recognize them if you saw them again?"

"Yes, I think so."

"What were their names?"

"I don't know."

"What did they look like?"

"They were about medium height, with dark hair and eyes."

"Is that all?"

"They spoke German."

"Remarkable. Two dark Swiss of medium height who speak German." He studied my passport for a moment, and then, his eyes half lidded, he looked up at me. "There was really nothing distinctive about these two Swiss?"

"No."

"Medium height, dark hair and eyes, spoke German."

"That's right."

"Why did you say Streicher went with them?"

"Because he was frightened that he might be harmed if he stayed here."

"What could he possibly fear?"

"I don't know," I said. "He worried about being mistaken for his twin brother, Adolph."

Guillot smiled faintly. "And so these two nondescript Swiss walked up to you on the Argentière glacier and said, 'Anyone who's afraid of staying in the Arve valley come with us.' "

"Not exactly," I said. "We met them near the—"

"Please, please, I have heard enough about these goddamned Swiss. Now, you were with young Dieter Streicher when he died."

"No, he was alive when I left him."

"Were there any dark Swiss in the vicinity? Still, you were present when this Dieter Streicher was hurt and Etienne Cottier was killed."

"That's right."

"Lightning," he said.

I nodded. "Lightning."

"You were on a very small ledge and lightning struck. Cottier was instantly killed, Streicher was injured, and you—you were unharmed. That seems a miracle."

"It happens."

"It seems a miracle to me."

"One man's miracle is another man's electrocution."

"A philosopher, a vagrant philosopher." He drew a breath and made a low humming sound in his throat. The humming lasted until he was out of breath and then he inhaled and said, "I will keep this passport. You will remain in this valley until I give you permission to leave."

"All right."

"You will report to me every morning at ten and every afternoon at four."

I nodded.

Guillot rose and came around the desk and walked me toward the door. I was very aware of his size. "You lied to me," he said. "God, you did lie! You didn't tell the truth at all. I am used to liars, but usually they try to weave some truth into the fabric of lies. But you—you're an insolent, contemptible liar."

I said nothing.

"Would you like to be more truthful now?"

"No," I said.

"I am personally offended by your lies. We French are

a very rational people—our Cartesian heritage, you know
—and you have insulted me with your irrational lies."
   "I had the feeling that you employed a little deceit
yourself, Guillot."
   "Come back tomorrow at ten and we shall talk again.
But don't lie to me anymore." And he slapped me hard
across the right side of my face. He put his full weight
into the swing.
   I stumbled backward across the room, hit the wall and
fell. My ears hummed. The humming turned into a shrill
whine and there seemed to be a causal relationship between the whining and the pain. I believed if I could stop
one, the other would automatically cease. I pressed my
palms against my ears, and gradually the whining faded
and the pain diminished in proportion. I rose slowly to
my feet. The door banged open and a very small, dapper
policeman entered the room. Guillot, hands in pockets,
was smiling at me in a friendly, affectionate way. I rushed
him, but the small policeman kicked my feet out from
under me, and I fell heavily to the floor. Guillot kicked
me in the kidneys with two precisely placed shots. I curled
up into a ball and fought against the reflex to urinate. I
believed I had succeeded, but when I slowly rose to my
feet I saw the dark stain on my trousers and felt the
warmth and smelled the ammonia odor of urine. I walked
between the uniformed policeman and Guillot, opened the
door and stepped out into the hall. I walked down the hall
with the stooped, painful shuffle of a sick old man.
   "Holmes," Guillot called, "the French Revolution came
before the American Revolution."
   I shook my head and kept walking.

The air outside smelled and tasted better than any beverage. I shuffled along the sidewalk to a bench and sat down. My face hurt and my lower back ached so badly that I had to double up. Passersby looked at me curiously. I felt as though a large part of my body had been made as sensitive as testicles and had then been smashed with a mallet. I hurt; Christ, how I hurt. I certainly was not going to lie to Guillot tomorrow. I was not even going to see Guillot tomorrow; I was going to get the hell out of this country. Tonight, and never mind the passport. At the moment I preferred to be an illegal alien in Switzerland than a legal resident of France. I did not want to become another victim of the famous French logic and rationality. The French logicked you to death in the same way the Germans metaphysicked you to death and the Americans killed you with generosity.

When I felt better I walked to a telephone booth and called Ted Fleming in Paris. There was a long delay and then he came on the line.

"Hello, old Holmes," he said. "How are things progressing on the Haute-Savoie front?"

"Ted, do I really work for you and your outfit?"

"Yes, of course. Didn't I say so?"

"You were pretty drunk."

"Yes, I was." And then in a sympathetic tone: "Holmes, I hope I didn't hurt you that night."

"What?"

"I don't recall much about the evening, but I do know that I pummeled you a bit. I expect you'd like another go one of these days."

"No, no, you whipped me in a fair fight."

"Well, I've done some amateur boxing, you know. It really wasn't fair of me to mix it up with you, even though you're quite a lot bigger than I am. Why are you Americans so big? Must be all those hot dogs and Coca-Cola."

"Ted, things are breaking fast down here."

"Still sleuthing, are you?"

"If I stay I very well may get into police trouble. How far will the company go with an employee?"

A pause, a soft clicking noise as if he might be tapping his teeth with a pencil. "Well, Holmes, you know that I *personally* would accompany you to the guillotine steps, but you're a new employee, actually, and the home office—"

"Okay," I interrupted. "I'm leaving France."

"Maybe if you told me what sort of trouble you anticipate. . . . And if you could indicate the caliber of the story. . . ."

"I resign," I said. "You owe me about four days' salary.

Forget the expenses—I'll collect them from *Paris Match* or *Der Spiegel.* Christ, yes, *Der Spiegel*—they'll pay me a little fortune for this. In marks, too; the soundest currency in the world."

"Listen, Holmes, if it's that interesting I'm sure the home office would consider providing first-rate legal counsel. And a bonus, of course."

"Two, maybe three pages of color photographs," I said. "Corpses stacked one atop the other like pancakes. Murder in the high Alps. I've got my lead, Ted: 'Hatred seethed in the hearts of the simple valley people for almost thirty years and then suddenly erupted into bloody retribution when the son and brother of an infamous war criminal—' "

"Holmes," he said disapprovingly, "that's pretty lurid writing."

"*Der Spiegel* can revise it."

"But you work for us."

"I just resigned. But I'll phone you from Switzerland tomorrow sometime. We'll discuss the possibility of re-employment then."

"You will call me, won't you, Holmes?"

"Probably."

"You will phone me, Holmes? I'll see what I can do."

"Mobilize the legal staff," I said. "Start oiling cogs and greasing politicians."

"It'd better be worth it."

"It will be."

"I'll do what I can."

"Do what you must, Ted," I said, and I hung up the telephone.

I liberated my motorcycle from a pride of dirty children and started up the valley toward the pension.

Martigny was still cutting hay in the field when I returned. I left my motorcycle beneath a tree and walked toward him. He kept working. He used the scythe with precision and economy, exerting no more and no less strength than was needed to perform the task. Every ten feet or so there was an hourglass-shaped bale of hay tied in the center with twine. I stopped a few feet away from him and watched him work. He did not pause or look at me. His brown face was slick with sweat and there were dark sweat patches in his armpits and crotch. Despite his mutilated hands he used the scythe well. I stood there for about five minutes and then finally Martigny surrendered. He looked up at me.

"You enjoy watching a man work?" he asked.

"If he works well."

He flicked the sweat off his forehead with the stub of his right index finger. His white hair was damp and spiky. He reminded me of an irritable old bear.

"And where is this Adolph Streicher?" he asked.

"You mean Walter Streicher."

"I know whom I mean. I mean Adolph Streicher. I have good reason to remember and recognize that man."

"Adolph and Walter Streicher were twins."

He looked at me. "That is stupid."

"It's true."

"That man was *Adolph* Streicher!"

"Twins. Ask Pierre Margolin. He knows."

"Why should I believe Pierre?"

I was infuriated by the man's slow, stubborn dumbness. "Because Pierre has investigated and inquired—he's not a thick-necked, thick-skulled peasant."

He surprised me by smiling slowly. Somewhere in his brain an entry was made next to my name, and only my extinction could erase it.

154

"Tell me, do you have peasants in America?"

"Yes," I said, "but we don't dare call them that."

He nodded, smiling.

"Jules, you killed Dieter Streicher, didn't you?"

"You're talking," he said.

"After I left you at the hut, you climbed the ridge, descended to the ledge, cut Dieter loose and pushed him over the side."

"I hear you," he said.

"It has to be you. I thought it might have been Alain Garnier, but he told me that when he arrived at the ledge the *choucas* had already gotten Etienne's eyes. That means Cottier's body had to be alone there for a time or else the ravens wouldn't have come."

"You are talking," he said.

"The chronology is clear—you killed Dieter, returned to the hut, and when Garnier reached the ledge, the ravens had eaten Etienne's eyes."

"I'm listening," he said, "but all I hear are mouth farts with an American accent."

"Adolph Streicher killed your son—you killed his son."

"Mouth farts."

"Who else have you killed recently?"

"Do you know what a guide is, Monsieur? I was a mountain guide for more than twenty-five years. My father was a guide, and his father too. My brother was a guide and three of my cousins are guides. I swallowed the ethics of guiding along with my mother's milk. The client's safety, that is all, that is everything, the client's safety—a guide will die to save his client. Go look at the museum exhibits and the guide cemetery if you don't believe me. That isn't necessarily heroism, Monsieur; it's a fact of nature, like that tree over there."

"You're talking," I said.

"A guide's first responsibility is to his client. And then, after that, the clients of his fellow guides. And then, anyone who goes into the mountains, anyone. It is dangerous up there, always. You know that; you're a climber. Your friends have been killed up there. You've come close to death. You know how dangerous they are, these mountains."

"I hear you," I said.

"Before they became guides my ancestors were chamois hunters, crystal gatherers, peasants. They ventured into the mountains, but not too far, not too high."

"I'm listening."

"Back then the mountains were dangerous, mysterious, ugly, horrible. Yes, horrible. But then the foreigners came here and they told us that the mountains were beautiful. And the chamois hunters and crystal gatherers and peasants began guiding these foreigners into the mountains. Look over there—are they beautiful, Monsieur?"

"Yes."

"Sometimes I think so too. Other times I see them as diabolical. Guiding, climbing became like war—the man next to you is a comrade even though you may hate him. But he is a comrade and so he is precious. My feet . . . these hands. . . . It happened in the winter of 1965. Some fools got caught in a storm on the Col de la Brevna. We had to try to help them, of course, even though they were fools. They were comrades too. The fools and two of the guides died, and I lost my toes and most of my fingers."

"I'm listening."

"I have killed," he told me. "During the Occupation I killed. I could kill again easily. Tonight, tomorrow—it's

156

nothing. But not in the mountains, my friend. Never in the mountains. Do you understand? That German boy—do you think I could kill that injured, helpless boy in the mountains? Ah, no, I could no more harm a human being in the mountains than I could change myself into a marmot. It's impossible."

"Mouth farts," I said. "With a Haute-Savoie accent." I turned and started away.

"Monsieur?"

I turned.

He let the scythe fall and held up his two mutilated hands. "The first joint of every finger is gone, you see. But these hands are strong. You observed the way I used the scythe. They are good hands yet. They are half the hands they used to be, but even so they are better than most complete hands. Strong. I am strong. I can work fourteen, sixteen hours a day every day and never become very tired. My heart beats thirty-eight times a minute when I am resting. When I work it beats fewer than sixty times a minute."

"What do you want, Martigny?"

"Christiane. You will not harm Christiane. Do you understand?"

"I have no intention of harming her."

"I am not talking about intention, I am speaking of results."

"I'm talking about intentions."

"She is a healthy young girl. Sex is normal—but I am warning you, Monsieur, she will not be harmed."

"Do you want to tell me your blood pressure now?"

"Good day. I have talked. Do not be surprised."

"I don't think I'll ever be surprised again."

I raided the kitchen for some cheese and two pears and carried the plunder up to my room. I stood by the window, eating and watching Martigny work the field. He went on at the same rhythmic pace and he never rested. He worked beautifully. It was almost an aesthetic experience to watch him. It was a kind of sweaty, masculine ballet. He was an agile bear, and I figured that he was just as tough as he claimed to be.

When it was dark I pushed the bed over against the wall and rigged my climbing rope around a bedpost. I opened the window and looked around. The moon had not yet risen; the woods and fields and buildings were just shadows of varying depth. A window glowed yellowly off in the distance. Doves rustled in their nests under the eaves. I threw the two ends of the rope out the window and then dropped my rucksack. The rucksack hit earth with a dull thump, and something inside clattered with the impact. I listened for a moment and then rappelled down the rope.

The ground was moist and soft underfoot. I pulled on one end of the rope at a smooth, steady pace and the other end came free, snapping against the windowsill and whispering through the air as it fell. I coiled the rope and tied it under the flap of my rucksack.

I pushed the motorcycle well down the road before starting it. The engine sounded unusually loud and rough in the silence of the night. I came to the end of the dirt road and turned right. I went through Chamonix and up the valley alongside the river which shone like viscid oil in the starlight, past all the little towns until I reached Argentière. I took the same trail out of Argentière that Streicher and I had used a few days before. The path curved through a wood and crossed a stream and then began tacking steeply up the hillside. The engine overheated. I could smell hot oil and hot metal. The headlight beam was like a bright round tunnel that I followed through the night. The engine stuttered and finally quit. It would not restart. I could hear nothing except the soft creaking of the engine as it cooled.

I adjusted my rucksack and started walking up the trail. Soon the salt sweat was burning my eyes, and my shirt was soaked through. A storm was coming: the night was much too warm for this season and altitude. The heat and exercise loosened my sore muscles and I walked at a rapid pace. I went up the switchbacks leading to the Lognan refuge. Lights glowed in the windows. When I was a few hundred yards away I left the trail and circled well below the building and then later picked up the trail again.

I forced the pace and paused only once, for a sip of water. My wool shirt was heavy with sweat. I used a flashlight at difficult parts of the trail, but then the moon rose above the high barrier of rock to the east and I did not need artificial light anymore. The moon was surrounded by a misty corona.

Then the path led more steeply downhill, and below

and to my left I could see the dim moonglow of the Argentière glacier. Another few hundred yards and I could smell it: a cool, damp odor, similar to the smell of the sea. I stopped to rest on the boulders of the lateral moraine. I had a taste of cognac and a little water and then I slowly smoked a cigarette. I was wholly alone. The night tasted of infinity. For a time I felt completely in harmony with the universe, but then I lost the beat and became an intruder again. I lashed on my crampons, shouldered my rucksack and stepped out onto the ice.

I hiked up the tortuous ice river most of that night. It was 2:00 A.M. before I reached the tributary glacier, and I needed another two hours to make my way through the steep icefall to the crevasse. I sat down on the snow and lit a cigarette. The stars seemed to have receded. The moon had given birth to another corona. The air was cooler now, but still it was too warm for this time and place. A storm was certainly coming.

I finished the cigarette and had a piece of cheese and some water. The glacier creaked. Somewhere toward the Aiguille du Chardonnet a sérac tumbled and thunder reverberated dully through the night. I dozed for twenty minutes, and when I awakened the moon was down and a few stringy clouds trailed across the darkened sky.

I had intended to wait until daylight to descend into the crevasse, but now I decided to go immediately. The weather was turning.

I placed three long tubular screws in the ice about eighteen inches apart and then connected them with a loop of nylon cord. I threaded the climbing rope through the loop and tossed the ends down into the crevasse. I slipped my arms through the straps of the rucksack, lit

the candle lantern and gripped the end of the chain between my teeth. The lantern dangled against my chest. I
could feel the heat rising and smell paraffin. I arranged
the rope in rappel position and backed over the side.
There was an awkward, dangling moment and then I was
inside the crevasse. It was the same. The ice looked like
glowing, green-blue glass in the candlelight. There was
a damp chill. The steps I had carved were still there,
slightly smoothed and rounded by melting and refreezing.
I reached the broken ice platform and stood there for a
time, experiencing déjà vu. I had stood in the same place
before and I was repeating certain actions, but more than
that, it seemed that all I would do this night had already
been done by me, and that I was capable of predicting
every mood and detail of the coming hours.

I walked over the jumble of ice to the ramp. I could
smell and taste the damp cold of the glacier. My crampons
bit into the ice with a crackling sound. The candle lantern
encapsulated me in its dim circular glow. The light drew
color from the ice, pale blues and greens and grays, and
threw my shadow against the east wall. The shadow was
a giant that walked a pace and a half behind me.

I reached the top of the ramp, put away the candle
lantern and withdrew my flashlight. My pulse and breathing rates had increased. I shone the light down into the
cavern. Streicher was sprawled out over the snow in the
same position as I'd last seen him. His corpse was dusted
with new powder snow. He was in the same position as
before, but fifty-some hours of death had effected a
change. The change could not have amounted to more
than a few centimeters here and there, but it was enough
to steal the last vestige of his humanity. He was just a

frozen carcass now. The carcass did not seem to have any relation to the man I'd known as Walter Streicher. His eyes did not reflect the light. Rictus and frost had contracted his lips into a kind of bucktoothed yokel grin. His eyes, his mouth, his rigid body—sprawled out on the snow as if someone had pulled a chair out from beneath him—had turned Streicher into something semicomical— the stereotype of a yokel laughing at another indignity. Nearby, two mismatched half-excavated legs stuck up out of the snow at impossible angles. The juxtaposition of complete corpse and two legs, centered in my flashlight beam, made the tableau appear both amusing and dreadful, like certain surrealist paintings. Sounds were trying to form in my throat. I did not want to hear them.

I carefully descended the ice ramp to the floor of the cavern. My breathing was amplified. Streicher did not have a yokel grin at this distance; it was more like a vicious sneer. The two legs stuck up above the snow— macabre flags.

I tapped a piton into the ice, lit the candle lantern again and hung it from the peg. Then, stepping between Streicher and the two legs, I walked ten feet down the gallery.

The glacier creaked like a door on dry hinges. I set my flashlight on a mound of snow and angled the beam toward Streicher and the legs. The candle lantern was burning, too, and the lights were reflected by the ice walls. The cavern was nearly as bright as my room at the chalet. The glacier rumbled with a sound like distant thunder.

I got my camera from the rucksack and inserted a flashbulb into the reflector socket. I took photographs of Streicher and the legs from several angles. I intended to record my excavations as carefully as an archaeologist would record his. The photographs might actually command a very high price in some European magazine or newspaper. They might also, in some way obscure to me now, provide evidence in my behalf.

I began digging around the upright legs with my axe. I used the sharp point to fracture the icy crust and then switched to the adze for the softer snow beneath. Chopping sounds echoed through the chamber. I could taste sweat on my upper lip. Every few minutes I paused to take another picture. When the bodies were completely excavated, I sat down on my rucksack and drank some cognac and smoked a cigarette. The stranger carried a passport which identified him as Michael O'Hara of Ireland. His body was as broken as Dieter's, and so it seemed probable that he had fallen from the great rock wall, too. Perhaps earlier in the summer he had been doing a solo of the same climb and had fallen. The ice slope above would funnel his body into this crevasse, although it seemed a bit odd that they had been found so close together.

I lit another cigarette from the tip of the last. Both bodies had been broken and then frozen into grotesque positions. Their limbs appeared to be jointed where no human joint ever existed. One of Dieter's legs turned at a perfect right angle several inches above the knee. His neck had been broken and his head—smashed like an old vase but contained by skin and membrane—looked directly backwards, like an owl. There was dried blood on their skin and clothing, and they were frozen as hard as the ice.

I exposed the rest of the film roll, taking individual pictures of Dieter and Walter Streicher and the man called O'Hara; and then I took several more pictures in which all three appeared. I felt as though I were intruding in a private tomb of blue ice. The corpses were not in any way a horrible or frightening sight, as I'd expected. That would have been better; that might at least have lent some dignity to life, if not death. But these broken, twisted, frozen dead looked like the victims of some sort of cosmic prank, and they had no more dignity than dogs run over by a car.

I gathered all of my things and cramponed up the ramp to the upper level of the crevasse. A misty rain was slanting down through the opening. It made silvery streaks in the lantern glow. The storm had arrived much quicker than I had expected.

The clouds had lowered to glacier level and mist crawled over the snow and settled in the hollows. Streamers of mist mingled with the rain. Somewhere along a ridge, high above me, thunder beat like kettledrums. Lightning flickered through the clouds. Even if it had been full daylight I would not have been able to see very far. Now, with dawn just beginning to roll back the night, I could see nothing.

Rain pattered against my nylon *cagoule*. I released the waist cord and unrolled it to full length. It fell below my knees now. It was shaped like a monk's robe and served as a kind of wearable tent.

I walked twenty yards and sat down in the lee of a big boulder. I decided to wait for a couple of hours to see if the storm continued. If it did I would have to return to

Chamonix. Conditions would become much too dangerous to attempt the long climb into Switzerland.

Half an hour later it began to seem as if the storm wouldn't last. Light seeped slowly down through the mist and became blurred and ghostly. The snow glowed like fox-fire. The air had a wet sheen, a slick gloss, and there was almost no transition between night and day. Sun warmed the mist and gave it an odor like sewage. The air stank. Mist condensed into dew. The air was so heavy with humidity, it seemed to me that I could reach out and wring water from it. For a moment the clouds opened and a great spear of sunlight angled down and illuminated the glacier, but the sky closed and once again I was immersed in the evil sourceless shine. And then I felt a breath of cool air. There was an instant when I could have extended my arms in a cross and felt the coolness on one hand and the humid warmth on the other. The wave of cool air enveloped me, and I could see my breath in the air. The rain changed into hailstones. They streaked down, big as marbles, drilling and pocking the snow, and I shrank back against the boulder and covered my head with my arms. The hail lasted a few minutes; there was a lull, and then big wet snowflakes began falling. Snow fluttered vertically through the dull luminescence.

I made myself as comfortable as possible and closed my eyes. There was better shelter within the crevasse, but I did not want to return there. I closed my eyes and waited, and waited; and then I dozed off.

I do not recall much about the dream. I was trapped on an enormous vertical rock wall. I saw myself from a distance, small, alone, helplessly spread-eagled on the granite face. Cracks radiated out from the center in a symmetrical and familiar form. I did not wholly recognize the form until I saw the giant spider rapidly descending from the upper left-hand corner of the wall—the web. The spider had almost reached me when I jerked awake.

I was still enclosed in the mist and snow. It was a complete whiteout; all perspective had gone mad. A five-inch-deep crack in the glacier became an abyss, a gentle rise now seemed a long hill, a thirty-ton sérac had been shrunk to snowball size by the atmospheric conditions. Objects receded while I watched, vanished, then reappeared again in a new aspect. Five feet was infinity. The mists boiled. Thirty feet became an arm's length. I had been in many whiteouts before, but nothing so weird as this. So I waited, still tense from the nightmare, trying to penetrate the baffling mists. There was danger here. I sensed it; I knew it.

A gigantic human form loomed up before me. It silently exploded into view, trailing vapor, parting the mists. The shape glided through the snowy cloud. It seemed weightless for all of its bulk; there was only the faintest crunching of snow. I closed my eyes for a moment, and when I reopened them the figure seemed a long distance away. It looked like a miniature person now, no bigger than a porcelain knickknack on a living room shelf. Snow fluttered down.

The mists spiraled and re-formed. The man became a shadow, a stain on the snow. There were sounds, but I could not identify the actions which produced them; sound was distorted as much as vision. It was maddening. I could not trust my senses. The physical world was lying to me and I was lying to myself.

The drab kaleidoscope clicked again and the dark stain

gathered itself up into a shapeless lump. It moved and drifted with the moving, drifting mists. I heard muffled crackling noises. A swirl of mist obscured the figure, and when the mists thinned he was gone. The magic of light and cloud was confusing, but I was certain that he had descended into the crevasse.

I got up and quietly walked in that direction. I had a feeling of vertigo. I would put my foot down and find the snow was six inches lower than it appeared. A few paces later I would lower the same foot and the glacier was six inches higher than I believed. The terrain was uneven, but it was the light that deceived me.

I almost stepped over the lip of the crevasse. It jumped up at me; it opened up out of the mists like great white jaws. I stepped back and then lay down on my belly. A rope, secured to a pair of long ice screws, led over the side. I crawled forward and looked down. I could see nothing, but obviously the man inside the crevasse could see me shadowed against the opaque sky. There was a sharp crack. It was not loud at first, but it echoed around inside the crevasse, increasing in volume until it became a hollow thunderous roar. Fragments of ice stabbed my face. I instinctively jerked back from the opening. The second bullet exploded a geyser of ice particles and then went whining off into the mists.

I got out my pocketknife quickly, opened the blade, slashed through the rope and tossed the end over the side. That would slow him down. He could climb the ice stairway I had chiseled into the crevasse wall, and probably do it with a pistol in one hand, but I had a few minutes' lead time now. I considered remaining there and killing him with my ice axe as he crawled up through the exit notch. There might be an instant when he was vulnerable. But he would understand that that was one of my options. He might choose to remain down there for hours. And he did have a gun.

I got up and began walking down through the icefall. It was like moving within a snowy, misty, dim globe of light. The world was reduced to a sphere some twenty to thirty feet in diameter, and even within that sphere all perspective was distorted. This was a complete whiteout, but I did not see how it could work to my advantage. I had to descend slowly, weaving in and out of the séracs, carefully skirting the crevasses or crossing them by snow bridges which might or might not collapse, while all the hunter had to do was follow my tracks.

A little later I paused and removed my sunglasses. It seemed to me that I could see slightly better without them. I estimated that I was no more than one hundred yards below the big crevasse now. It had taken me twenty minutes to go that far. He would be able to cover the distance in half that time. I looked back. My footprints were slowly filling with snow, but it would be hours before they were completely covered. The hunter would be out of the crevasse soon. He might be following my trail right now. I had made a stupid mistake. I should have remained by the crevasse and killed him when he emerged. I thought about returning, and then immediately rejected the idea. The only thing to do was to keep running.

I went on, and a few minutes later a dark shape suddenly rose up before me and to my left. The shape moved at a right angle until it intersected my path. I raised my ice axe and rushed toward the shape, but it was only a boulder lying in the snow, and its motion was an illusion caused by the blowing mists. I looked back. The footprints at the farthest limit of my vision seemed to be moving too, jumping around like small dark animals. The glacier was an *Alice in Wonderland* sort of world where, with the connivance of my fear, boulders acquired grace and mobility and footprints turned into frolicking animals. And though I knew I was moving down a steep slope, it appeared almost level—the light, the mists flattened everything. Panic began moving inside me, climbing, scratching at my throat. I had been in danger many times, but this was a new reaction. It was as though something that had always lived placidly inside of me had concluded that my body was no longer a refuge, and it was moving, scrambling, clawing to get out. What chance did I have in this insane environment against a killer (I was sure it was Martigny) who was so much more familiar with the terrain than I was, and who had all the advantages in this fox-and-hare chase through the snow?

I went on, moving faster now, taking more chances. I descended through the icefall maze, hearing sounds, seeing shapes, now in flight as much from phantoms of my mind as from the actual danger.

I blindly stumbled on for an hour more, turned north toward the green valley, rushed on through the mist and snow and ice for almost two hours, until gradually my panic began to seep away. I was still alive. I seemed to have opened a good lead—perhaps I could win at this game after all. Panic had taken me swiftly down through some very dangerous terrain, and in that respect it had been an aid; but there was no hope of continued survival unless I began thinking quickly and clearly.

I got out my compass, released the needle and waited

impatiently for it to stop swinging. It was hard to believe. The compass indicated that I was traveling in a southerly direction, when all along I'd been certain I was heading north. It couldn't be. It didn't make any sense. Over the years I had developed an acute sense of direction; the whiteout could not have confused me that much. I moved away from my ice axe and rucksack, away from all the metal gear that might affect the compass, and took another reading. It was the same. But, Jesus Christ, how could you believe you were moving downhill when actually you were gaining altitude? I *had* turned to my left —north—at the juncture of the two glaciers, but then I must have gradually veered off to the east, and then south, beginning the curve of an enormous circle. That was a tenderfoot stunt. That was the reward of panic. And so now, instead of being below the hunter, only hours away from safety in the valley, I was lost in a whiteout on one of the most difficult glaciers in the Alps.

Where was Martigny now? He knew this glacier nearly as well as an ordinary man knows his own neighborhood. He could be below me, waiting—or following my tracks in the snow, perhaps smiling to himself as he began to realize that, like the greenest of the green, I had been running in a circle. Either way, he was to the north, blocking my egress to the valley.

That was my only possible exit. To the south and east and west were the great barriers of rock and ice and snow. The snow slopes would be avalanchy now. The rock would be covered with *verglas*. And the higher one climbed, the worse the weather would be. It was difficult enough to climb out of this granite amphitheater even during the best of weather; now, in the storm, it was virtually impossible.

All right. The thing was to remain calm and rational, to survive until night and then hole up somewhere. Then my options would increase from none to three or four. The storm might continue and cover my tracks, and I could remain hidden for a day, two days, three, until Martigny gave up. Or perhaps I could slip past him in the stormy darkness and make it down to the valley. The glacier was wide enough to make such an escape feasible. Or, with a few hours in which to think and prepare, I might be able to trap or ambush him. Or, when the weather improved, I might attempt to climb up out of the basin and escape onto one of the other glaciers. I needed time, though; the next few hours were crucial. And, of course, it was now imperative that the storm and whiteout continue.

I looked at the watch I had taken from Streicher. It was almost two o'clock in the afternoon. I had been running from Martigny much longer than I'd thought; my fear had compressed time. That was good. I had only about five hours until night. If I could evade him for just five or six more hours. . . .

Fox-and-hare it was, then. I retrieved my rucksack and started off again, thinking now, using my trail to confuse and delay and, I hoped, to destroy. I arbitrarily awarded myself a fifteen-minute lead. If I was able to add five minutes per hour until nightfall, I would accumulate a total lead of forty minutes—enough, I thought, to make escape a certainty.

First it was essential to deceive the fox. If I was compelled to play the part of hare, then I would simply have to be one hell of a devious hare. I proceeded to lay out a crazy maze of tracks. I doubled back on my trail, established false leads, created loops within loops within loops, walked up a long, avalanchy slope to a rock wall and climbed a hundred feet of icy rock, and then traversed another hundred feet along a broad ledge before descending again to the glacier. I crossed a snow bridge over a long, wide crevasse and then destroyed the bridge with my ice axe. I curved my trail around every sérac I could find so that Martigny would have to move very slowly in fear of ambush; walked backward down my own tracks and then went off in another direction; leaped a narrow, snow-covered crevasse and then removed my right boot to make a footprint in the center of the depression (let Martigny believe it was safe to cross there); created more loops and angles and confusion. I did not expect every deception to work, but if just a third of them did I would have gained the time and space I needed.

It was about six o'clock when I heard the gunshots. There were two of them, sharp whip-crack snaps which were immediately followed by a series of dull, diminishing echoes. For an instant I felt totally surrounded by gunfire. The noises came from every direction. But the initial cracks originated well to the north. It was difficult to estimate distance in the echoing amphitheater, in the snow-and-cloud-muffled storm, but I calculated that Martigny was still several hundred yards below me.

I had sufficient lead time now. But the most encouraging thing was that Martigny was being frightened by shadows. Perhaps he had seen a boulder glide menacingly across his path, or footprints leaping and tumbling. The strain was affecting him, too, and now he was shooting at specters in the snow.

18

For the last thirty minutes before total darkness I looked for a sheltered space where I could bivouac the night. I moved slowly through the smoky dim globe of light, and just as I was resigned to spending the night in the open, I found a crevasse that would do. Rather, the crevasse found me. I was walking over what appeared to be a safe, level stretch of ground when suddenly the snow at my feet collapsed and I was falling. I saw the hole open at my feet; then the glacier seemed to rush up toward me, reach eye level, pass overhead; and I was inside the crevasse, falling. I anticipated death with a kind of bitter detachment. So it was my turn now.

I struck bottom almost instantly. My legs jackknifed and I was pitched forward against the ice wall. I lay there, stunned, for some time, and then I slowly began testing my body. My left ankle and shoulder both hurt, but it did not seem that either had been broken or badly sprained. I looked up toward the circular hole in the snow roof. I had fallen only eight feet, rather than the two-hundred-plus feet I had expected.

I removed my rucksack and got out the flashlight. I was at the east end of the crevasse. It was small, about fifty feet long, eight feet deep and about the same in width at its broadest point. The walls were concave, shaped like brackets, and closed at bottom and top except for the hole I had made falling through. I might encounter some difficulty getting out in the morning.

There was a pile of powdery snow beneath the area where the roof had collapsed. I buried my ice axe, spike-end-up, directly beneath the hole and then hand-shoveled snow around the shaft until the spike was covered by about two inches of snow. Anyone jumping down through the hole had a fair chance of being impaled.

I gathered my equipment and walked down the oval corridor of ice. The ice was milky colored in the beam of my flashlight, and a few wraiths of mist clung by their tails to the walls and floor.

I started to light a cigarette and then stopped. If the hunter was close, a whiff of cigarette smoke would be enough to bring him down on me. Nor could I use the little butane stove to brew tea. I did not think he was that close. I guessed that he was still some distance away, now doing the same as I was, preparing his bivouac. He could not sleep, though. He must force himself to remain awake during the night, listening, peering into the darkness, sensing. . . . He could not permit me to slip past his "lines" during the night and escape back to the valley. Nor did I believe he would attempt to track me down until morning. My trail was too complex to unravel in the dark, even by flashlight.

I decided to rest until about three in the morning and then try to slip past Martigny and run for the valley. I hoped the whiteout would last all night.

I removed the half-length sleeping bag from my rucksack and pulled it up over my hips. Then I got out a piece of cheese and a tin of sardines and ate them slowly. I alternated between bites of the sharp cheese and the oily fish. When I finished eating, I used some of the olive oil as an ointment for my chapped, split lips and sunburned face. The ultraviolet rays of the sun had burned me through the cloud cover.

I tried to sleep but I could not. My mind remained alert even though my body was exhausted. I was still full of adrenalin.

Light had ceased filtering down through the hole in the crevasse roof. It was totally black in my ice room now. I was tired, cold; I had burned many more calories than I'd consumed during the past day and a half.

The glacier creaked softly. I moistened my lips and face again with the olive oil. My eyes were dry and gritty. It felt as if finely powdered glass lay beneath the lids. The luminous dial of Streicher's watch glowed a blurry green in the darkness. I listened to my heartbeat and the rapid ticking of the watch. I listened, and then the ticking turned into a deafening mechanical clamor, the grind and clang of giant cog wheels turning in imperfect synchronization.

I awakened several times in the darkness, shifted around to increase circulation, then again slipped off into a shallow, chilled sleep.

Finally I was awakened by the pain in my eyes. I had been dreaming that a shadowy figure had been burning my eyes with bright jets of flame, and the pain remained with me after the nightmare receded. I sat quietly in the cold darkness, exploring the limits of my agony. It felt as if my eyes had been melted into jelly. The pain was excruciating: it was localized, and yet it sickened my entire body.

I commanded my eyes to open. They disobeyed. I commanded again, and I could feel the fluttering of my eyelids, a flood of tears on my cheeks, but I could see nothing. I fumbled in my pocket for the little steel match cylinder, removed a match, struck it against the roughened side of the cylinder and held it aloft. Tears, a dim, foggy radiance that vanished when the match went out. Snow blindness.

I was nauseated from the pain and the knowledge of what this meant. Ophthalmia. In this case, a burn of the corneal epithelium. I had removed my sunglasses yesterday morning during the whiteout. The sun had not been visible yesterday, but its ultraviolet rays had penetrated the mists and then reflected off the ice and snow. The thinness of the air at this altitude, the reduction of a filtering effect, plus the great reflector basin of the glacier had combined to blind me. It was the same sort of blindness you can get by staring too long at a welder's arc. It was temporary; it usually lasted from two to five days and did not result in permanent eye damage. But that was no comfort now. I might just possibly last several days in this crevasse under optimum conditions, but I was being hunted, and Martigny would find me shortly after dawn. I was blind. I could not even run. All I could hope for now was that it would snow again and my tracks would be covered by fresh snow.

I got out my pocketknife, opened the smallest blade and then very slowly and gently pried off the crystal of Streicher's watch. By exploring the dial with my fingertips I could learn the time. It was now a quarter to three.

It was not long after dawn when he came for me. I became aware of his presence by a soft hissing sound, the faintest of whispers, as a thin stream of snow poured down through the hole in the roof at the opposite end of the crevasse. He was apparently standing by the hole, and his weight had triggered a tiny avalanche. The hissing stopped. I opened my eyes and stared down the ice channel. All I could see was a dull, grainy mist. Pain and tears forced me to close my eyes.

There was silence for perhaps five minutes, and then finally, in French, he said, "I know you are still down there."

"Yes, Martigny," I said. My voice was dry, but strong enough.

"Why are you still here?" Martigny asked. His voice echoed down the tunnel of ice.

"I'm blind."

"Ah, yes." A pause. "You should never remove your dark glasses on a glacier, never."

"I really don't require any mountain-guide-lecture bullshit, Martigny."

"Well, I am almost sorry it happened this way. I was enjoying the hunt. You were very clever."

I did not reply.

"This has been like the war days, this contest."

"Listen, Martigny," I said. "Understand. I'm not begging. Go to hell. Kill me or not, but listen—if you'll let me go, I'll never say a word to anyone."

"I would like to believe you."

"The Streichers are dead. There's nothing I can do about that. Sending you to the guillotine won't help them. Take me back to the valley and I swear I'll never say a word to anyone."

He was quiet. I visualized him standing on the snowy glacier, his gun aimed down through the hole in the crevasse roof, waiting, maneuvering to commit murder. I saw him against the kind of pure deep blue sky that follows a storm. I had tried to live like a man, and I wanted to die like a man, but the thought of that sky almost broke me.

"Martigny, I mean it. I'll return to America. I swear, I won't forget, but I'll never mention it either."

"There is no advantage," he said.

"There is the advantage of not having another murder on your conscience."

"I have no murders on my conscience."

"The Streichers."

"That was not murder. I executed Adolph Streicher to help redeem the honor of France."

"You killed Walter Streicher, not Adolph. And why did you murder Dieter Streicher?"

"I killed the boy out of loyalty to my son's memory."

"Christ, you employ big, noble words to rationalize low, slimy crimes. Honor and loyalty."

"Yes."

"Did you know, Martigny, that the motto of the SS was 'My honor is my loyalty'? Lofty words. But listen, if you kill me—will that be out of honor to France or loyalty to your son? What will you call that? I'm blind; I'm helpless. If you come down here and shoot me, it's a cold vicious murder. You won't find any pretty words for it."

"I'm sorry," he said.

And then he jumped down into the crevasse. I had forgotten about the ice axe. Martigny screamed. It sounded more like the scream of a cat than a human: it was a prolonged, throaty, hoarse shriek that trailed off into a whining keen that raised the hair of my arms and neck. The crevasse amplified and echoed his screams. He screamed that way, and then, breathing rapidly, he said "Oh!" on each exhalation—"Oh! Oh! Oh! Oh! Oh!" Then I heard a dull implosion of breath followed by the queerly pitched nasal keening. The sound rose into a kind of whistle and then abruptly ceased.

"Martigny?" I asked.

Just his accelerated breathing, snuffling inhalations and exhalations that sounded like the soft grunting of a bear. He breathed at a fantastic rate, perhaps one hundred or more times per minute. Gradually his breathing rhythm slowed, although it was still much faster than normal, and it was loud in the echo chamber of the crevasse.

"Martigny," I said.

"Oh, God," he said. "Oh, Jesus God. Oh, hail Mary, full of grace. . . ."

"Martigny. Maybe together, working together, you understand—maybe we can get back to the valley. Your eyes and my legs, Martigny."

"No," he said.

"We can try it."

"Don't talk," he said. "Please. I'm trying to crawl outside of the pain."

"Where did it get you?"

"Abdomen," he breathed. "The snow collapsed . . . just as I jumped. I fell forward . . . oh, Jesus Christ, I think it went through me."

"Do you still have your gun?"

A long pause. "Yes."

"You're lying. It's out of reach or buried in the snow."

"I have it."

"No," I said.

"Come for me, then."

"Maybe I will," I said.

We did not speak for almost an hour. The crevasse was filled with his harsh breathing and the aura of his pain. Then he said, "Get me a priest."

"There are no priests out here," I said.

"Please, a priest."

"Have you forgotten where we are, Martigny?"

"I must confess."

"If confession will give you solace in dying, then confess to me. But I can't absolve you of anything."

"Did I do wrong?"

"Yes."

"Am I damned?"

"I can't say."

"It was easy to kill Adolph, easy—but the boy. . . . I didn't even intend to hurt the boy. I went down to the ledge to help him until the rescue team arrived. I gave him Coramine, glucose, brewed him tea—two cups of tea— warmed his hands with my hands. And all the time I looked into his eyes and saw my son, my Jean. Jean didn't look like him, but that is who I saw, Jean. But then, then I looked at him and saw his father. He had the same jaw and eyes as his father. Adolph killed my son. It was . . . I couldn't . . . it was like a dream. I cut the ropes that belayed him."

"Christ," I said.

"He didn't understand. He didn't know what . . . and then I pushed him over the side. I was watching myself do this from above and from a distance, as in some kind of dream. I was observing myself and him. Just before he went over I became myself again. He looked at me and . . . his eyes weren't Adolph's anymore. His eyes begged me. His eyes begged; God, how they begged! But he didn't speak. He didn't even scream as he was falling."

Martigny paused. "It was easy to kill Adolph. That was not a sin."

"You killed Adolph's twin, Walter Streicher."

"No."

"Yes."

"Please," he said. "Get me a priest."

"We're on the glacier, Martigny. And I am blind."

He was silent for a long time, and then he said, "Ah, mon Père, vous êtes venu."

I said nothing.

"Mon Père, j'ai péché."
I remained silent.
"S'il vous plaît." His breathing was getting shallow. *"Je meurs, ne me refusez pas ça. Confessez-moi."*
"This is Holmes," I said.
"Je vous en prie, mon Père." In his delirium he believed that I was a priest.
"Ne me laissez pas mourir sans . . ."
I crawled down the narrow ice gallery until I touched something that was not ice or snow—Martigny's shoulder.
"Mon Père?"
I could smell blood and excrement. He had defecated.
"Ecoutez ma confession, je vous en prie."
Many years ago I had covered, as a young reporter, the aftermath of a hurricane that had devastated the Louisiana coast. I'd spent most of one night in the company of a priest as he visited the injured and the dying and the dead, and I had heard him repeat, dozens of times, certain ritual words which I had never forgotten.
"Mon père?"
What I intended to do was probably wrong, but the man was dying.
I said, *"Ego te absolvo—"*
"Ah, merci."
"—a peccatis tuis—"
"Merci, merci."
"—in nomine Patris et Filii et Spiritus. Amen."
Martigny's breathing seemed easier then. I sat by him for perhaps a half-hour, and then suddenly his entire body stiffened. He went rigid. I tried to scramble away down the ice tunnel, but he grabbed the front of my jacket, and then his grip quickly slid upward and he had me by the throat.

His mutilated hands were terribly powerful, even as he was dying. His thumbs pressed into my trachea. I thrashed around in total panic. I struck him on the face and chest with both of my fists. His grip tightened. There was a noise in my ears like the ringing in a seashell. Colored lights flashed before my blind eyes. I struck him lower, in the abdomen. The ice axe was still in him. My fists were wetted in his blood. I twisted and levered the ice axe until he released his grip on my throat. I crawled ten feet away and lay there quietly as the ringing in my ears subsided. My throat hurt, but he had not broken the trachea. I tried to scrub the blood off my hands with snow. I could not hear Martigny's breathing now.

I did not think that he had deliberately tricked me. I believed that he really had been delirious toward the end, and that his contrition was genuine. But he had lived with hate too long to die in peace. Hatred had become a part of his chemistry. It didn't matter whom he thought he was killing, if he thought at all during those last few moments —Adolph Streicher, me, someone else. His last reflex had been violent.

I crawled over to the body and found his wrist. There was no pulse. I dragged the body partway down the crevasse, away from the hole in the roof, and then went through his rucksack. I found some bread and cheese, water, a stove and fuel, and half a dozen capsules—probably glucose.

I returned to my bivouac site. Now I simply had to survive until my vision returned.

20

The chief threat to my life now was hypothermia, a critical lowering of body temperature. Heat was life. The calorie was my unit of exchange: I would have to balance intake and expenditure with a miserly economy. I tried to recall all I had learned about hypothermia. You lost heat through radiation, conduction, convection and evaporation.

The radiation loss would be minimal. I had good down clothing and a small, sheltered place in which to stay. The snow roof over the crevasse would help reduce the degree of nighttime radiation loss.

Conduction. Heat flows from the warm object to the cold, and the larger the variation in temperature, the swifter the transfer. My *cagoule,* the foam pad, the rucksack, Martigny's clothing and equipment too, if necessary, should provide adequate insulation between my body and the snow.

Convection. Again, well-designed down clothing and protection from wind and water should minimize heat loss due to convection.

Evaporation. I simply could not afford to sweat. When I became chilled I might exercise to increase my metabolic rate, but I absolutely had to stop before sweating commenced. Too much heat is lost through sweating, and a cycle begins that sometimes cannot be halted. I would also lose some heat through the natural drying of the skin and through respiration, but that could not be controlled.

The potential heat loss through any single one of them, radiation, conduction, convection or evaporation, was not too serious, but their cumulative effect over several days might kill me.

On the plus side I had some food which, if carefully rationed, might provide my body with enough heat energy to stay even for a couple of days. I had two stoves, my own and Martigny's, and sufficient fuel. I could raise my body temperature through the introduction of hot tea, soup, water. Even the stove flame during cooking periods would help a little. Nicotine causes vasoconstriction, and so I could not smoke.

It was going to be close. I wouldn't win or lose by much.

There was a secondary problem. The crevasse, almost entirely enclosed, would reveal only subtle variations of light; but I was blind and I would not even see that much —I must live in total darkness for several days. I would be deprived of the stimuli of light and color and form.

The temperature in the crevasse would remain fairly constant no matter whether it was blazing hot or numbing

cold up on the glacier surface. I had to survive for days
at a temperature of about thirty-two degrees, and so I
would also be without the stimulus of climatic change.
And there would be no sounds here except my breathing
and the creak and thunder of the glacier. What could I
touch? Myself, my equipment, ice and snow. And scent?
Ice and snow, my body. As for the sense of taste, I had
a little tea, some honey and rye bread, cheese, three packages of dehydrated soup mix, candy, and a half dozen
capsules which I assumed were glucose. Enough to fuel
my body, perhaps. But still, I was blind, virtually deaf,
practically without the senses of smell and touch, and
alone.

I had read of experiments in which men, by a variety
of means, had been deprived of all external stimuli, and
even the strongest among them had begun exhibiting per-
sonality disorders within nine or ten hours. I was locked
inside the most cruel prison imaginable—the penitentiary
of the self.

I wound the watch and then gently explored the dial with
my fingertips. It was 9:25. The second hand was moving.
The watch had not been damaged during my struggle with
Martigny. That was lucky. I would have to be very careful
of it. Without a crystal the hands could easily be bent or
broken. The watch was my only real link with reality.
With it, I could calculate my place in time, see in my mind's
eye the position of the sun and moon and stars, fix a point
in the future when I would be free of this sepulcher of ice
and snow. Each hour that passed brought me closer to that
arbitrarily selected future moment when, no longer blind,
I would crawl out into the world. The watch ticked, and
those ticks were my transportation from point A to point

B. Without them I might become hopelessly lost in the stagnant timelessness of infinity.

The daylight hours passed easily enough, mostly because I knew that it was daylight. I ate and drank small amounts at intervals; played with my memory, re-creating the grass and skies and lakes and winds of childhood; sang songs; slept. I should not have slept. I was not tired enough then to sleep when night came (and I knew when it was night because the watch dial told me so). The temperature inside the crevasse did not alter noticeably, and yet I became chilled. Light did not diminish for me—I was blind; but I felt immersed in a new and deeper blackness. I could no longer imagine the sun brilliantly reflected off the ice and snow, the warmth, all the great white mountains around me and the wonderful blue sky. Instead I saw shadows, icy starlight, frozen forms and desolation.

During the night I continued to eat and drink a little; mentally worked out problems of arithmetic; dueled with fear; encountered remorse on my excursions into the past. And I slept some, too, in the late hours.

Finally the watch dial told me that it was morning again. I was warmed by a vision of the sun; my heart opened and expanded into all the vastness of the sky.

The second day was more difficult. I ate and drank the rations I had assigned myself at the designated times; explored the past and the future; advanced into algebra. The watch hands moved slowly.

The dial informed me of twilight, and night. I ate and drank more than I should have. I ate and drank; ventured into geometry; quarreled with friends and family and strangers about abstract topics. I employed different voices for my various opponents. This did not impress me as

194

being abnormal—I thought I was enduring the mental strain quite well. I slept, and exercised to regain warmth, and slept again. Finally I awoke and touched the dial of my watch, and I knew it was morning and Mont Blanc's summit was ablaze with light.

"The sun! The sun! The sun!" I chanted, until my voice was hoarse.

Later I removed the bandage from my eyes and I shouted. For an instant it seemed that my vision had returned to normal. I could see Martigny's body, lying twisted on the crevasse floor fifteen feet away from me, the cool blues and greens of the ice, a dazzling shaft of sunlight that slanted down through the opening. And then my eyes flooded with tears and the pain was so intense that I almost fainted. I soothed my eyes with snow and then covered them with the bandage.

I sat there all day in apathy. I did not eat, or dream, or think. I recall nothing until the moment many hours later when I touched the dial of the watch and realized that my fingers were numb. My toes too were completely without feeling. I placed my hands inside the down jacket beneath my armpits, and after about a half-hour they began to tingle and burn as circulation returned. When my hands were warm I removed my boots and massaged by toes until pain told me that they were well again.

The small capillaries in my hands and feet had closed. When your temperature decreases beyond a certain point, the body begins taking action to sacrifice the extremities in order to preserve the vital organs. Frostbite is the result. Frostbite and then gangrene and then, if you are lucky enough to be still alive and medical attention is available, amputation. My health was deteriorating.

I fumbled with the stove and boiled some dehydrated soup and drank it so hot that it burned my tongue and throat. I drank two cups of soup and ate some rye bread with honey and then boiled some water for tea. My morale as well as my temperature lifted with the warmth and nourishment. Tomorrow, surely, my eyes would be well enough for me to cross the glacier to safety.

That night was the worst of my life, an unrelieved anguish. I was cold, so cold, and despairing, and time became my enemy. Each second seemed to stretch elastically, reluctant to separate from the one preceding and the one to follow. I began to think fondly of death. I ate and drank. I massaged my toes and beat my hands against my thighs. I waited. Finally, toward dawn, I slept.

On the morning of the fourth day I was awakened by sounds, the dry crunch of snow, a voice.

The sounds came nearer. "Jules?" the voice asked. "Jules?" It was Christiane and she was very close, probably at the opening of the crevasse. "Jules!"

"Here!" I shouted. "Christiane, I'm here, in the crevasse!"

A silence and then. "Robert?"

"Yes."

"Where are you?"

"In the crevasse, to the west. Do you see the opening? Jesus, I'm glad to hear your voice! How did you find me?"

"The tracks—I've been following tracks in the snow for a day and a half. My God, what tracks! What are you doing down there? Can't you get out?"

"I'm snow-blind."

"For how long?"

"Three days."

"Three days! Are you all right otherwise? Have you seen Jules? I've been looking for Jules."

"He's down here."

"Oh, thank God! Jules. Jules? Is he hurt? Why doesn't he answer? Jules!"

"Christiane, Jules is—"

"I'm coming down there."

"—dead."

"What? Jules is—what did you say?"

"He's dead."

"Oh, no."

"I'm sorry, but he is dead."

"But he *can't* be dead."

"He tried to kill me."

"What? What? Jules tried to kill you and he's dead?"

"Yes."

"Oh, God! I'm coming down there."

"Wait! It's ugly, Christiane."

"Did you kill my Jules?"

I quickly removed the bandage. My eyes were glued shut; a crusty substance had sealed the lashes together. I had to force my eyelids apart with my fingertips. I could see light and shadow and form, but hazily, as if in a fog or whiteout.

"I didn't want to kill Martigny," I said. "I had to."

There was a scraping noise and I looked down the misty gallery of light and saw a dim shadow falling downward. There was the sound of an impact, and the shadow crumpled, remained motionless for a moment and then rose again. My eyes were streaming water now. My cheeks were wet, and my vision was further distorted by the lenses of water covering my eyes. Christiane, a blurry

197

shadow surrounded by a foggy aura of light, advanced toward me. I rubbed the water from my eyes. I could see her more clearly for an instant, but then a new flood of tears threw the crevasse into a dim, underwater perspective. I was certain that she intended to kill me. Perhaps she had found Martigny's gun. But then the wavering, haloed shadow stopped and knelt on the crevasse floor beside that other shadow, Martigny. "Ah, father, Jules, father," she crooned, and then she wept softly for a long time. She wept, then she stood erect, and her voice was not softened by grief.

"You did this to him?" she asked.

"I set a trap with the ice axe. He fell on it."

"You did this to *him*?"

"I had to."

"You are nothing!"

"He was a murderer."

"You trapped this honest, honorable man as if he were an animal!"

"The son of a bitch *was* an animal!" I shouted furiously. "Won't you listen? He pushed that poor goddamned Dieter off a ledge and buried an ice axe in Walter Streicher's head! Your sweet, beloved, mourned Jules pushed an injured man off a ledge two thousand feet up; and I am simply so Jesus Christ sorry you don't think it was sporting of me to set a trap for him; and you can just take your haughty ass and turn it around and start back to the valley, because I can walk out of here alone and unaided."

"I will take you back to the valley," she said quietly.

I said nothing.

"If you will agree to my conditions."

"I can get out of here by myself."

"You fool. You look like a kitten that has just opened its eyes."

"I'll be able to see better tomorrow."

"A storm is coming."

"I don't care."

"You fool, you, die. You're as proud as Jules was."

"Martigny wasn't proud, he was mean."

"You never knew him. He was a fine man, a great man, once."

"And what the hell kind of person are you to negotiate terms over my life?"

"I'm not a very nice person," she said. "Like you."

"What's your deal?"

"I'll lead you back to the valley and in return you will not involve Jules in any of this."

"No."

"He's dead now. What good can it do to make him known as a murderer?"

"How can it harm him?"

"No. You'll do as I say or I'll leave you here to die. Believe me, I swear before God I'll walk home alone if you don't do this thing for Jules."

I hesitated. "I'll do it for you, not Jules."

"Jules Martigny went alone to climb. He was caught in a storm and he vanished. That is all. He died in his mountains."

"Guillot is after me."

"I know Guillot. I can talk to Guillot."

"Do you think he would cover this up?"

"You leave Guillot to me."

I wanted to see her face. I wiped my eyes again and peered down the oval of ice, but her features were still only a pale blur.

"All right," I said.

"Good."

"I'll try it your way. But the minute I'm called before a magistrate, I'll tell the truth."

"That's all I ask."

"That's all you demand, baby."

"Put on your sunglasses. You don't want to injure your eyes any more. Here, I'll help you gather your things."

"What about Martigny?"

"This is a better grave than most."

"Christiane, listen. I didn't want to kill him, I swear. I tried to talk to him and—"

"Please!" she said. "Oh, please, don't ever talk to me about it, not any of it."

It took us fourteen hours to return to the valley.

21

I remained in the hospital for three and a half days. The doctor told me that I had one of the worst cases of ophthalmia he had ever encountered. I also had a touch of frostbite on my left heel and two of my toes; nothing serious—white patches which later turned violet and later still peeled away like badly sunburned skin. I wore a slipper on my left foot and walked with a limp for about ten days.

Captain Guillot and a police stenographer visited me during the afternoon of the second day. My eyes were covered and so I could only picture Guillot in my mind: big, slow moving, with his lidded eyes and mismatched lips. He prowled around the hospital room as he talked, and even though I could not see him, I turned my head in the direction of his voice.

"Mademoiselle Renaud has confided in me," he said.

"Has she?"

"It is necessary, for the record, to possess your statement on certain matters."

"Of course."

"Not that Mademoiselle Renaud and I do not trust your word or your discretion."

"I understand."

"But, hypothetically, if you were to make some sensational allegations in the press about events which may or may not have taken place in this valley, allegations which might, let us say, malign a certain highly respected, now deceased member of the community—well, we should like to produce a document signed by you which contradicts such allegations. Do you see?"

"I believe I do."

"Good. The stenographer will begin recording. Ready, Victor? Now, I expect, Mr. Holmes, that you will cooperate in this inquiry?"

"I certainly shall, Captain Guillot."

"Splendid. I believe you are a truthful man."

"Thank you, sir. I try to be." I pictured Guillot's slow, ironic smile.

"Is there anything that you wish to report to the police regarding recent activities which you believe might be violations of the criminal codes and statutes?"

"No."

"It is rumored that you have made accusations. . . ."

"I was mistaken."

"Perhaps," Guillot said. "Perhaps you can tell me what happened to the two Streichers?"

"Well, I don't know . . ."

"You don't know?"

"I can only speculate."

"Speculate for me."

"Well, it seems . . ." I paused, wishing I could see Guillot's face.

"You did tell me in a previous interview that Walter Streicher had crossed into Switzerland. I have that talk recorded on tape. Remember the pair of dark Swiss who spoke German?"

"That's right."

"Do you maintain that he left the province, the country?"

I hesitated. "What do you think, Captain Guillot?"

"It sounds logical. But only you know for certain."

"That is precisely what happened."

"Then there is no necessity to concern ourselves with Walter Streicher's whereabouts. He voluntarily left France, according to your testimony. And the young Streicher—Dieter—what do you suppose happened to that lad?"

"Well . . ." I said.

"It has come to my attention that you believed he was murdered."

"I was mistaken."

"You really were?"

"I was exhausted, I was . . . upset."

"Ah," Guillot said.

"I was confused."

"Yes. The guide Alain Garnier believes the boy either committed suicide by rolling off the ledge or he was swept away by an avalanche. What do you think?"

"I lean toward the latter view."

"Just another unfortunate mountain tragedy, an accidental death."

203

"Yes."

"And his remains are now buried deep in some inaccessible crevasse."

"Probably."

"And Jules Martigny. What do you suppose happened to poor Jules?"

"I can only guess, Captain."

"Guess for me, son."

"I believe he must have been caught in the recent storm while attempting a difficult solo climb."

"And he perished alone?"

"I can't conceive of any other explanation."

"Do you have anything you'd like to add?"

"No." I did not think it would be wise to introduce the mystery corpse, Michael O'Hara of Ireland, into this interrogation.

"Now. Have you been subjected to any physical or psychological intimidation or duress during this interview or any previous interviews?"

"Absolutely not."

"You state that without qualification?"

"You have been most courteous, Captain."

"Is this your truthful and final statement?"

"It is."

"The stenographer will leave the room and type up copies of our colloquy. Do you have any objection to signing them?"

"None at all."

"All right, Victor," Guillot said.

I heard the scrape of a chair and then the sound of the door being opened and then closed. Guillot was silent for a few minutes and then he said, "Is this your camera on the dressing table?"

"Yes."

"I'm taking the film."

"All right. After this statement I'd have a hell of a time explaining those pictures."

"Exactly." I heard him open the camera case. "Pierre Margolin sends his felicitations," he said.

"When did you see Pierre?"

"This morning."

"If you see him again, will you ask him to visit me?"

"Monsieur Margolin has left the province."

"Oh."

"I suggested that since the weather here is unfavorable, he might more profitably study the flora of the Dauphiné Alps."

"I see."

We were silent for perhaps five minutes, and then the stenographer returned and I was directed to sign the three copies.

"I can't read them, as you know," I said.

"They are an exact record of our conversation," Guillot said.

"I'm only a moron, Guillot, not an imbecile." I pressed the bedside buzzer, and when the nurse arrived I asked her to read the statement. It had been translated into French but remained an accurate rendering of our talk. I would not be signing a confession of complicity in the Dreyfus case or of attempting to steal French atomic secrets or of accepting responsibility for the loss of French colonies. The nurse left the room, and Guillot directed my hand to the bottom of the pages and I signed them.

"Thank you," Guillot said. "Incidentally, one of my men retrieved your motorcycle from the mountains above Argentière. It's down in the hospital parking area now."

Before leaving, Guillot suggested that the next time I chose to climb in the Mont Blanc massif I might prefer to establish my base in Courmayeur, Italy. I agreed that there were a lot of climbs on the Italian side that I had not attempted. It might be years before I returned to Chamonix. It could be a lifetime, he said.

The next morning the doctor removed the dressings from my eyes. My eyes were still sore and sensitive to light, but I was assured that my vision would be as good as before. Then would it be all right if I read my mail and the newspapers? Yes, but I should not read for too long. Could I leave the hospital today? Well, no. . . . It really would be better to wait one more day. . . . Tomorrow, certainly.

The following morning the doctor returned and dilated my eyes with some drops and then studied them through his ophthalmoscope. His breath smelled of bacon and he made noises deep in his throat. Finally he switched off the light.

Was everything okay? Yes, fine, fine, though I should wear sunglasses while outdoors for a few days. Could I leave the hospital today? Of course, of course; right now if I wished.

There was a smell and taste of autumn outside. The air was tartly cool and the leaves of the deciduous trees were turning gold and scarlet and mauve. Migratory birds were hysterically swarming over the roofs and fields. A blue wood smoke haze hung above the valley. Above the haze the mountains, white with new snow, rose up steeply until they were finally halted by the hard blue infinity of sky.

I drove my motorcycle west through the valley and then turned left on the dirt road which led to the Martigny pension. I stopped the bike beneath a tree next to the creek and turned off the engine. Christiane was picking apples in the orchard. She glanced at me once and then resumed working.

I walked through the dust and sunlight and then into the cool, sweetly rotten-smelling shade of the orchard. There were apricot and plum and cherry and apple trees there, but only the apple trees were still bearing fruit. The ground was loamy-soft underfoot. Patches of blue sky flashed through the dark tangle of branches and leaves overhead. Christiane turned and watched me as I approached. There was no expression on her face. She was wearing sneakers, tight, faded Levis, an old blue denim shirt. A red bandana covered most of her hair.

I stopped next to the bushel basket. "Hello," I said.

"Hello."

I took one of the apples from the bushel and bit into it. It was small and hard and bitter. I threw it aside.

"We use them for cider," Christiane said.

"Is the cider good?"

"It's all right. The fermentation sweetens the juice."

"How are you, Christiane?"

"Have you come for your things?"

"I came to see you."

"Well, here I am," she said, and she lifted her arms and pirouetted coquettishly. "What do you think of my ensemble?" I could see that she felt as awkward as I and was trying just as hard not to show it.

"Your ensemble is a symphony in blue and red," I said.

"Chic?"

"Très chic."

"It's all from the fall collection of Monsieur Levi Strauss."

"Do you hate me, Christiane?"

She let her arms fall. "Ah, no," she said.

"Will you come with me to Paris?"

She shook her head.

"I really would like you to be with me."

"We would be like cats and dogs."

"Well, let's try."

"No, Robert, really, but thank you."

"What are you going to do?"

"Leave here."

"Did Jules have a will?"

"It seems not."

"Were you ever legally adopted?"

"No, I don't believe so. No."

"Will you inherit this place, then?"

"I think so. Jules had no relatives."

"Christiane, somewhere Jules has a third cousin or a niece by marriage, and you'll hear from him or her. Relatives are going to swarm here like crows to carrion."

"Really, Robert, I don't care. Really. If this place *is* mine I'll sell it and emigrate to Canada."

"Property is worth a great deal in this valley."

"If this place is not mine I'll use my savings to emigrate. Either way, I'll leave here, and France, and Europe."

"Even so, you've earned all of this."

"Robert, you don't *earn* anything with love."

"Someone must," I said smiling. "I've always *paid* quite a lot."

"I must start all over. I want to become a child again somewhere new, and then grow up into someone a little different."

"Where will you go in Canada? Québec?"

"Yes. A friend of mine married a Canadian five years ago and she's a *Québeçoise* now. We've written all these years."

"But Christiane, if you go to Québec it won't be a completely fresh start. You have a good friend there; you'll be speaking French. The customs, the food even, will be similar...."

She stood quietly for a moment. "You may be right."

"I certainly am right. I'm an expert at fresh starts."

"I'm so tired. Maybe I'll go to western Canada. Or to the United States, or Mexico. I just don't know."

"Well, baby, good luck."

"Sure, baby," she said, smiling.

We went into the chalet and upstairs to my room and I collected all of my belongings. We were very aware of each other in the room: this was where we had made love that night, and while it hadn't meant much to either of us at the time, it seemed to be one of those small incidents that, in reverse perspective, grow larger and larger as they recede. Sometimes they grow so big with the years that you can't see anything else.

We went downstairs again and out into the sunlight. I packed all of my things into the motorcycle's big saddlebags and then we kissed briefly—she smelled like apples —and then we said goodbye, smiling, be sure to write someday, goodbye, maybe we'll meet again in the New World, smiling, goodbye Christiane, goodbye Robert, smiling and touching, hang tough baby. I started the bike and turned it down the dirt road and before turning into the trees I waved without looking back.

I went west on the valley highway and twisted the throttle until I was going seventy miles per hour. Fields,

trees, houses, sky, the river, mountains, flashed by me.
I went around a truck filled with hay, a Renault and then
a Volkswagen. The autumn air was cool on my cheeks.
The sky and mountains shone as they must have shone
ten thousand, twenty thousand years ago. I went on
through Les Houches and then around a corner and past a
sign which read:

```
         vers

       ANNECY
        PARIS
       GENÈVE
```